The Keeper's Secret

Diane Doona

Pont

Published in 2015 by Pont Books, an imprint of
Gomer Press, Llandysul, Ceredigion, SA44 4JL

ISBN 978 1 84851 966 4
ISBN 978 1 84851 967 1 (ePUB)
ISBN 978 1 84851 968 8 (Kindle)

A CIP record for this title is available from the British Library.

This book is published with the financial support of the
Welsh Books Council.

Printed and bound in Wales at
Gomer Press, Llandysul, Ceredigion

To my daughters,
Mel and Manda,
for whom I originally wrote it
all those years ago.

Chapter 1

I knew something was up that day. I came home from school to find Dad standing in the middle of the floor, looking decidedly flustered and surrounded by piles of half-packed boxes and cases.

'Hey, what's up?' I said. 'Are we going away?'

Now why hadn't I thought of that? Perfect! After everything that had happened, a holiday would do us both good.

'Erm, no ... not exactly ...' came Dad's reply. He turned away from me and pretended to look busy. Something's going on, I thought.

'Sooo, what's with the packing?' I was puzzled.

Dad looked at me. He didn't answer, just stared vacantly into space. He'd been doing a lot of that lately.

'Dad?' I was losing patience.

He gave a deep sigh.

'We're moving,' he said bleakly, 'I've sold the flat.'

Then he looked away again, with a sad and guilty expression all at the same time.

'MOVING? Where to?' My voice was all squeaky and high-pitched. I hated it when it went like that.

But this was unexpected; I mean, he hadn't even mentioned …

'Oh, you mean somewhere *smaller*?' I guessed, desperate. I tugged his sleeve; this was serious.

'Wales … we're moving to Wales.'

'WALES! No! Dad, I don't want to go to Wales. We live *here*, in London! What about school, my friends? Dad please …' I squeaked. But he just looked away, with a heavy sigh.

'It's all arranged,' he said with dreadful finality, turning back to his packing.

And that's where the conversation ended, because I fled to my room slamming the door behind me, and by the time we left a week later I still wasn't properly speaking to him. My life was turning upside down; nothing was the same anymore.

First Mum, and now this.

*

I sat with my head turned towards the window, the rain making millions of crazy rivers on the glass. I watched them snaking their way down; sometimes they paused in mid-run then continued their jerky journey in a watery race to the bottom. I had my sulky look on; it sat stubbornly on my face and refused to budge.

I avoided eye contact with Dad, but from the

corner of my eye it was easy to see his sadness. I'll admit that made me feel a touch guilty, but leaving behind everything I'd ever known seemed pretty unfair to me. I didn't know anyone in Wales, and I didn't want to either. We'd have nothing in common and, worse still, what if they all spoke some crummy Welsh language or something? My mood was black, but there was no way out of it; we were moving. Still, that didn't mean I had to be nice about it.

We'd left early, at first light, and the train had limped out of London, clunk-clacking noisily through the crazy mish-mash of tracks which surrounded the city. Leaving London was like leaving Mum behind, even though she wasn't there anymore, but it was where she'd been with us. That thought sat in my chest like a lead weight as we headed west.

If I'd known then how things were going to turn out, I guess I wouldn't have been quite so moody.

As we ventured further west the buildings and factories gave way to green fields, where black and white cows paused mid-chew as if they resented the noisy train disturbing the peace. Cotton-wool sheep stuck like fuzzy-felt to the sides of the hills and, well, I suppose it *was* quite nice, but in my mood I'd already made up my mind that it was all pretty boring. The rain gradually stopped and a weak

February sun shone through the window. I must have nodded off, because the next thing I knew was Dad tugging my arm.

The tiny station was a fair way out from Manorbier village, which seemed funny to me – what was the point of having a railway station if it wasn't on your doorstep? Maybe that was the way they did things in Wales.

We took the only taxi in sight. No black cabs here, just an old battered Renault. The roads we took seemed little more than tracks they were so narrow. I swear if we'd met another car we'd never have stopped in time. We held on for dear life, and I couldn't help myself – I caught Dad's eye and my face broke into a grin. That kind of broke the ice a bit and, to tell the truth, a little bit of me was glad. Dad deserved a bit of happiness after everything, and I felt my bad mood begin to disappear, as I made up my mind to try and be nicer. Well, most of the time anyhow, depending on how this whole Welsh thing turned out.

It was as we zoomed round the final bend into the village that I caught sight of a grey shape looming in the distance. It was the castle Dad had told me about – except I hadn't really been paying attention at the time, I was too busy sulking. Then the taxi pulled up in front of a small cottage – our new home.

Chapter 2

I opened my eyes with a start and looked at the gnarled wooden beam above my head. It took a moment to remember where I was. Was I dreaming? I shook my sleepy head. The creaky old bed squealed as my feet touched the floor, as if it wasn't used to being woken that early.

After dumping our bags in the cottage the night before, Dad and I had headed up to the village pub for a meal. Listening to the chatter of locals, I was pretty relieved that not a word of Welsh was spoken. I managed to grasp some words, though they spoke with an unusual twang which I had never heard before. A man at the bar explained that Pembrokeshire was known as 'Little England Beyond Wales,' and that there was very little Welsh spoken here – especially below the Landsker, he said. Apparently that's some kind of invisible line which separates the Welsh-speaking north of the county from the south, where Dad and I had come to live.

Under my breath I thanked the Anglo-Saxons – apparently that was all their doing. Even so, the man's accent was rough and he spoke so fast I could hardly understand him. He said '*like*' at the end of every sentence, which made me want to laugh. If all the kids at my new school spoke like this then I was in trouble, I thought to myself. Then we'd walked back down the hill to the cottage, the bare trees making eerie black patterns against the darkening sky. We chatted quietly as we walked along. I felt close to Dad then, and it was like old times, and it made me miss Mum a lot.

My room was small, a bit pokey, with a low, beamed ceiling; not much room for all my stuff. With luck the pink flowered wallpaper would soon be a thing of the past; Dad had already promised to repaint in my own colour choice, and I intended to hold him to it. Nothing wrong with orange in my book! I picked my way through the assortment of bags I'd dumped on the floor and crossed over to the window, sniffing the cool air which smelt sharp and salty. I could hear the sound of waves crashing on the shore and I liked the idea of being so close to the sea. I could see why Dad had chosen this spot; it might be the ideal place for him now.

I leaned out as far as I could; it was still early and a light mist draped itself over everything like a veil. It seemed to glow in the thin morning light. I could see the tip of a church tower and some distant rooftops. Over on the right the mist was much thicker and it was impossible to see anything.

I yawned, wondering what time Dad would be up. Then, just as I turned from the window a patch suddenly cleared in the thick white mist and I glimpsed the battlements of a castle. Then the mist swirled again and it was gone.

A shiver ran down my spine. I shrugged it off.

Downstairs I heard Dad filling the kettle. I threw on some jeans and a sweater, stopped by the mirror to pat down my mop of unruly black hair, which was something I did every morning if I didn't want to look like a hedgehog all day, and went to join him. London seemed a billion miles away and suddenly it didn't seem to matter. Something told me this was where I was *meant* to be. Weird eh?

Yep, I settled in to my new life surprisingly fast … then everything changed when I met M.

*

Later that morning a van arrived with the rest of our stuff, bits of furniture that Dad was particularly fond of. I suppose they'd been Mum's favourites too. The big blue toolbox and crates of books, the TV, the mountain bikes and lots of other stuff were all dumped inside the house. Strapped on top of the van was Dad's old kayak; he'd had it for years and we meant to try it out as soon as the weather warmed up.

Our little cottage was set in its own walled garden and was completely white both inside and out. It made a perfect picture against the hillside. It sure was a far cry from London. Creepers curled themselves around the front door and the porch was filled with potted plants. Thinking back now, I wonder how they survived with just Dad and me to look after them. Mum had always been the green-fingered one in our house.

We wandered up to the village shop and bought some supplies, enough to last us a few days. We would need to make a journey into town soon to stock up with other stuff we needed. We studied the bus timetable by the village hall and noted the times.

Dad kept me busy that first day. I guess he thought it was time I pulled my weight, so while he hacked away at a pile of rotting tree trunks at the bottom of the garden, I filled up the wheelbarrow and piled the logs he'd cut into a neat stack under the eaves of an old shed in the far corner. Once we'd found places for most of our belongings, we stacked the rest of the boxes in a tidy pile in the hall for another time.

The day turned cold and windy. Dad lit a fire in the stone fireplace and I remember watching the flames leaping and dancing, their shadows flickering on the walls. I hadn't felt this good in a long time and I began to think things would turn out okay after all. It was almost as if we were back to normal, though more often than not, I still saw that faraway look in Dad's eyes. It was something he just couldn't hide.

After a supper of bacon, sausage and scrambled eggs, followed by buttered teacakes and mugs of tea, we sat close to the fire and I asked Dad to tell me everything he could remember about his visits to Manorbier as a small boy. He dug out a couple of books from one of the unpacked boxes and we studied the pictures inside. My interest was caught by a plan of the interior of the castle and the story of the de Barri family who built it way back in mediaeval times. I decided that a visit to the castle would be first on my agenda.

That night I lay in bed and thought about everything I'd learned in that book. When the Normans invaded this part of Wales they'd had an eye for the best spots on which to build. The castle stood proud, on a hill above a wild, rugged coastline, just a stone's throw from the little sandy cove. With its strong towers it was a brilliant point from which to spy any invaders.

I felt reassured. But why did I suddenly think that mattered now? There were no invaders now. There was nothing to threaten this sleepy little village anymore.

But I couldn't settle; I tossed and turned, churning things over in my mind, until eventually I fell asleep and dreamt I was sailing a tall-ship in the little bay. I was all alone in a wild and violent storm – then I heard a noise above the pounding of the waves; a wail, a pitiful cry, so sad it stayed with me till morning when I woke in a tangle of sheets, bathed in sweat. It was hours before I could shake off my anxiety. That dream was to return to me time and time again in the following weeks, disturbing my sleep, and I wondered what it could all mean.

Chapter 3

The next Saturday I left Dad building bookshelves; he'd brought so many books with him I wondered where they'd all go, but I guessed when he eventually went back to work, he'd need them all. Anyway, he said they felt a bit like old friends and he could never get rid of them. He seemed a bit more cheerful that day, so I decided to go exploring.

I found the track Dad had told me about. I remember it was a beautiful sunny day, more like April than February, and I whistled as I cycled along. Everywhere was deserted, quiet as the grave. The path wandered through a copse, where the sound of birds nesting filled the air. I stopped to watch a bold blackbird collecting twigs before it disappeared inside a tangle of ivy. It was unreal to think that a week ago I'd been in London with its congested streets and pavements.

Then unexpectedly I stumbled out onto a road, which led onto a wide gravel driveway, and the castle entrance was there right in front of me. I'd been to far bigger, grander castles than this one, as well as countless stately homes and palaces. That's what you got for having a Dad like mine, who's obsessed with history. But this one felt different. A right old mismatch of broken towers and crumbling walls mostly covered with creepers, it loomed against the deep blue sky.

I threw my bike against the hedge and made my way down the drive. I love those old doors you get on ancient mediaeval buildings; the wood twice as thick as your arm, and this one was a beauty. I ran my hands over the grainy wooden planks and stared down into the deep moat, dry and overrun now with stubborn weeds and spiky grasses. The drawbridge was held strong by thick iron chains and I thought of all the souls who'd crossed over it. If I closed my eyes tight I could almost hear the clash of hooves on stone, the chink of armour, shouts of '*Whoa there!*' as riders on mighty steeds clattered through the entrance.

There was a small sign pinned to the door telling me the castle was closed till Easter, but I decided to walk around the outside anyway. It was hard going as there was no path as such, and I couldn't get through much of the bushy growth, which had grown up around the back. Still I carried on. Something was drawing me to this place; I felt a deep connection with it that I couldn't explain. It all felt very strange.

So there I was, sitting on the wall chewing at a nail when I heard the sound of footsteps crunching on the gravel. Then this girl strode round the corner and came to an abrupt stop when she saw me. She stood there with her hands on her hips, a scruffy dog at her heels. I can remember even now the way she looked that day, the sun lighting up her brown hair, turning it golden. I always liked the way she wore it in one long plait snaking down her back, unruly curls escaping. For years I never saw it any other way. She threw a dark accusing look my way. The dog pricked up its ears and eyed me too.

Now, I wasn't used to such bold scrutiny, particularly from some girl I'd never even met. Before I could stop myself I felt the heat rush to my cheeks; I knew they'd gone all red and blotchy. They always did that. I decided to walk right past her and just grab my bike. But what was intended to be a casual, confident stroll ended up with me performing a clumsy un-orchestrated kind of ballet, my legs flying in all directions and my arms flapping up and down for dear life as I skidded on a patch of loose stones. With one hand I tried to grab the wall and steady myself, but it was she who swooped forward to stop me from falling flat on my face.

Our faces were inches apart. Our eyes met. Hers were dark brown, almost black, clear, intelligent eyes; mine that unremarkable murky grey like the colour of seaweed, always drifting off somewhere – or at least that's what my teachers used to say. I swore she was laughing at me behind that innocent face. All I had to do was grab the bike and leave. But I hung around – erm, don't ask me why.

'It's closed,' she said, in a *"you're an idiot"* sort of voice, flicking her head towards the castle, so that the plait swung to and fro like a pendulum on a clock.

'I know.' My voice sounded defensive. I wasn't completely stupid. I almost added 'I *can* read,' but that might have seemed rude and I didn't want to spoil things straight away; she might just turn out to be okay. I turned my back on her and reached for the bike.

'You on holiday?' she asked, just a shade friendlier.

'No.' I offered no further explanation. That would annoy her!

'You're not from round here!' she frowned, hauling the plait over her shoulder and fiddling with the end of it.

She had a way with words and she lost no time in finding out where I came from, what I was doing there and where I lived, though I didn't tell her the whole story until much later … that was much too personal. On the other hand I learned almost nothing about her that day, 'cept she'd been born in the village and had lived here all her life. From the way she spoke, with a fierce kind of pride, I could tell she loved the place though.

The sun slipped low in the sky when at last I bent to pick up the bike.

'So, what's your name then?' she demanded, seeing I was about to leave. As I replied I fondled Pepper, the dog, and he licked at my hands like an old friend. I decided to like him. As for the girl ... well, I still hadn't made up my mind about her.

'Joe,' I said.

'Joe ... Joe what?'

'Joe Jackson.'

'Well Joe Jackson, I gotta go now ... see you around maybe.'

'Sure,' I said.

I straddled the bike and she walked along beside me until it became obvious she was heading in the other direction. I hoped we'd meet up again, but I didn't say so. I hadn't gone very far when I skidded to a stop.

'Hey,' I yelled, 'you didn't tell me *your* name?' She turned, raising her arm against the vivid red ball of sun just beginning to slip below the horizon.

'Just call me M,' came the short reply.

'M?'

'Yeah.'

'Just M? What's it mean?' I was puzzled.

There was a long silence.

'M ... my name's M, okay ... that's what everyone calls me.'

It was a good while before I found out what the M was for.

Chapter 4

Of course I soon saw her again, at school a few days later. She was in my year and I soon learned that she was pretty smart at most subjects, though she kept herself to herself; that was obvious.

School was a far cry from what I'd been used to. Going to school for me had been a taxi ride through the clogged up streets of London from our swanky Georgian terrace in Notting Hill. We'd lived in a street where just about every other house was a clinic or a surgery, where people came to have their teeth polished or to change the shape of their bodies. But Dad was a historian and spent his time researching or giving talks at schools and universities and other places, mostly in and around London. He'd written a couple of history books too. Sometimes I'd get a lift to school with him if he was going in my direction, but more often than not he worked from home.

As for Mum ... well, Mum worked strange hours, and would often be long gone from the house by the time I left for school. I didn't get to see her or spend time with her as often as I'd have liked, but I was proud of her. Some people would say she shouldn't have done what she did, but I guess Mum always did what she believed was right. And that's what helped me get through it all. I wished Dad could do the same.

The school was about a mile outside the village and most days I rode my bike or took the school bus if it rained, which it never seemed to do that often, at least not in those first few months. Or maybe that's what happens to people's memory when they get older; they look back and think that every day was long and sunny.

I soon settled in. I make it sound easy, but it wasn't, not all the time anyway; the other children were naturally curious, and asked questions I didn't want to answer. But M seemed to sense my reluctance to talk about the past so she never asked. We'd amble home together, me pushing the bike. She soon began calling for me at the cottage on Saturday mornings, often with Pepper sniffing at her heels. Sometimes she got talking to Dad and I could tell he found her interesting too. Or maybe he was just pleased I'd found myself a friend, which meant I wasn't hanging around bothering him.

Looking back I wonder what we did with ourselves – before everything happened, that is. February turned to March and the weather was unusually warm. Mostly we'd end up just sitting and talking, sometimes down on the rocks in the bay, or in the fields around the cliff path, or just hanging around the village on our bikes. We spent hours down on the shore, poking sticks into rock pools to see what we could find. I never tired of it. It was a happy time, and one of healing for me. M was a mine of information; she knew the names of each and every tiny creature, where they lived, what they ate, and what ate them. I lapped it all up.

It was during these times that I learned a lot more about M. One particular day we were back sitting on the old crumbling castle wall when she told me how her granny had been a traveller, moving from place to place all her life. Her mother was barely sixteen when she found out she was having a baby. She gave me a kind of sideways look with those black eyes when she said this, but I said nothing. I wanted to hear more. That was when her granny decided to settle down; she'd had enough of people trying to move them off the land and she'd always loved the sea. So that's how M came to be born in Manorbier and although she had never met her father she told me that that didn't bother her one bit, she was perfectly happy living without one.

I wondered if I could be perfectly happy without a mother.

We would often sit on the little wall by the castle where we'd first met; it was one of our favourite places. It was there that we first had the idea. Or at least M did – she was always the one with the bright

24

ideas. She told me she knew a secret way into the castle. It was her idea to meet after dark, when there was nobody around.

Dad kind of assumed I was over at M's place and I guess her mother thought she was at mine. I felt guilty about deceiving Dad, but he was so wrapped up in himself in those days, it seemed easier just to do my own thing. He never seemed to question where I was or what I was up to. He'd taken to going for long walks along the cliff path by himself, and when he wasn't doing that he'd just sit by the window, an unopened book on his lap, staring out, as if Mum might walk through the gate at any minute. To my mind it was just a harmless bit of adventure. What could possibly go wrong?

Chapter 5

It was a cold night, the air snappy with the threat of frost. A chilly breeze moved through the trees and I imagined they were whispering to me as I made my way along the track. I didn't meet a soul.

The sky was lit up with zillions of tiny, shiny stars and I kept stopping to stare up at it. We'd hardly ever seen stars in London; there were just too many streetlights there.

I felt a bit nervy; my throat was dry and scratchy, but I didn't let on. M was her usual cool self. Nothing seemed to spook her, not even creepy castles in the dark. The castle looked magnificent that night, standing in the light from a pale moon, which hung like a huge silver coin suspended over the battlements. I drew in my breath and shivered. It was crazy, but it seemed like my whole life had been spent waiting for this moment to happen.

'You scared?' said M, sensing my mood.

'N … no-o … I just, I dunno. Feels weird, that's all.'

She raised her eyes at me, a look I was getting used to by then, and shrugged. Then, pointing over to the left side of the castle where there was a thick patch of scrubby undergrowth against the walls, she set off. I followed close behind. We kept our heads low. The ground smelt rich and earthy, like old boots. Then, just as we reached the undergrowth she seemed to disappear right in front of me. I couldn't make it out; one minute she was there, then …

'Joe, over here.'

On my left I could just make out her pale face in the half-light, poking through from a small gap in the wall, which had been hidden behind an outcrop of fallen stones. How had I missed it? I wriggled through behind her, and found myself on a narrow ledge leading onto a flight of stone steps.

Even now I remember that moment as if it was yesterday. It was breathtaking. The towers loomed above me creating dark shadows, which seemed to shift and move whenever a cloud drifted over the moon. I felt small and insignificant, like an ant, as I gazed up at them silhouetted against the starlit sky. The air smelt sharp and I breathed it in in big mouthfuls.

I followed M across the ledge onto the steps and then down onto a wide sweep of grass with soft rolling banks. We headed for one of the arched doorways, which led up to the battlements. We stayed close together, cautiously at first, keeping in the shadows; then wandered up tiny, winding stairs, up and up, until we reached the top. From

27

there we could gaze at the sea, the moon's reflection shimmering on its surface, and the waves crashing on the shore in a sparkling mass of frothy foam. Then we tottered back down the narrow staircase again, only to climb up another. At ground level there were several large square rooms; we tiptoed from one to the other on soft earthen floors. Somehow they still smelt of long ago, damp and muggy, and I recognized the chapel from the plan in Dad's book.

M tugged at my arm and flicked her torch on the wall where there was a bold black sign with white lettering; 'The Dungeons.' An arrow pointed ahead to an arched opening. The light from our torches seemed pretty feeble as we aimed them into the deep inky blackness. And then we stepped inside.

The thick air hit the back of my throat and I felt the hair prickle on the back of my neck. My heart was pounding like crazy. I could hardly breathe and I staggered sideways. M threw me one of her looks then motioned for us to go back outside. I slumped down on to the grass feeling useless and stupid, but I was as weak as a kitten. M stood over me, hands on hips again, just like the first time I'd seen her.

'What's up with you?' she hissed.

But before I could answer there was a noise, a kind of snuffle coming from inside the arched opening. I swear my bones turned to jelly. The snuffling sound came again. Slowly, almost mechanically, we began to back away, unable to take our eyes away from that dim, dark doorway. Then, shuffling out of the shadows, a dark figure came towards us, and not far behind it was another shape, much bigger, and I had no idea what on earth that could be. M pushed me back and threw herself beside me. We flattened ourselves against the wall as best we could.

'What ...?' I began, but she silenced me with one of her fiercest looks, begging me not to utter a sound. Something told me we hadn't been seen yet. I wished a cloud would come along and hide us in its shadow.

'What is it?' I whispered, my voice shaking.

'Shhh, I don't know ... but ... it's ... it's coming closer,' her voice came out in a raspy whisper. I heard her suck in her breath. As for me, well I don't think I was breathing at all.

For what seemed an age, we stayed stock still, our backs pressed hard against the wall, neither one of us daring to move, though I guess deep down I just wanted to take to my heels and run. I looked across the grass to the gap in the wall. It looked a long way. But I think I'd lost control of my legs by then; I couldn't have run if I'd tried. I gasped out loud as the two of us were suddenly flooded in blinding torchlight.

'Well, well,' said a voice, deep and rough-edged.

The light from the torch was dazzling and I couldn't see a thing.

'Oh, Mr. Barrow, it's you. You gave us *such* a fright, we thought ...' M's voice trailed off lamely.

'Well, young lady ... and what might you be doin' here this time o' night, eh?' a voice replied.

An ancient-looking man emerged from the dark shadows. His head was bent so low I couldn't really see his face. He wore a battered old oilskin coat and a checked cap on his head. I couldn't speak but I was searching the darkness behind him. It was strangely quiet now. There were no more snuffling sounds and I began to think I had imagined it; that the other shadow I had seen was just the light playing tricks. The old man's cap was pulled forward. All I could glimpse was a thick grey moustache and a stubbly chin.

Suddenly he looked right up at me with sharp eyes which were deep and strangely luminous ... kind eyes I remember thinking. I returned his look with a steady one of my own, and I felt a strange connection with him, as if I'd always known him. Then he spoke again and it was as if his question was directed straight at me.

'So, what d'you make o' my castle then, young 'un?'

At that precise moment the moon appeared from

behind a cloud and lit up the battlements in streaks of silver light.

'It's beautiful … amazing,' I stammered, feeling self-conscious, barely able to find my voice. M shivered beside me.

'Please don't tell …' she began.

I stayed silent, still peering into the blackness beyond, not really sure what I was looking for.

And then I heard it, that snuffling sound again, coming from the shadows behind the old man.

I swear my knees almost buckled beneath me. I strained to hear and there it was again, and I knew M had heard it too as she threw me an anxious look.

'Er … we should be going,' she stammered, tugging my sleeve. Her voice sounded thin and hollow.

The old man looked slightly uncomfortable, shifting from one foot to the other. Then clearing his throat, he put a reassuring hand on M's arm.

'Wait,' he said, 'now don't be alarmed, no 'arm'll come to you, I promise.' He paused, and then carried on muttering as if to himself.

''Tis a blessing, 'tis a blessing. 'Tis right. Time 'as come, as I prayed it would. You two be the ones, aye, I'm sure o' that now.'

His eyes seemed to bore right through me as he went on.

'Can feel it … 'tis right. Aye, 'tis time, 'tis time.'

As I listened to his mutterings I felt as if I was under a spell. I couldn't move. My legs were like lead weights. Whatever this was about, I knew I had to find out. Then the old man seemed to pull himself together and looked straight into my eyes. It was hypnotic. My heart hammered inside my chest.

'I knows you two can be trusted,' he continued, 'but 'tis late. Go 'ome now, and come back next week, on Sat'day, same way's you come in tonight, like. Come at three ... and you'll learn the whole story then ... aye, the whole story. 'Tis best you knows it all, like,' and with that he turned on his heel, and we heard the unmistakable snuffling again, as he disappeared inside the dungeon. As he shuffled away I couldn't help noticing that in complete contrast to the clothes he was wearing, he wore a pair of threadbare tartan slippers on his feet.

I stepped forward, as if to follow him; it was M who grabbed my arm and pulled me back. Silent and subdued now, we made our way over to the steps and on to the ledge. We scrambled through the gap in the stones and it wasn't until we'd reached our wall that we spoke again. We sat there, shivering, hugging our coats around us. M told me what she knew about the old man.

His name was Jasper Barrow. He was the castle caretaker, and had been as long as most people could remember, and he lived on his own in a small cottage in the very shadow of the castle itself. People said he'd been there forever. Seemed like he kept himself to himself most of the time.

It was a good half hour later that we reluctantly parted at the top of the drive and I jogged down the hill towards home. My thoughts were in turmoil. What was the old man hiding?

The week stretched ahead and I was frustrated – I was certain we'd come close to learning something amazing; but why did I think that? I didn't know anything; had only been in the village a matter of weeks. It was puzzling. It sounds weird but I felt certain there was a message somehow meant for me – but that sounded just a bit too farfetched, so I said nothing to M about it. She already thought I was a bit strange and I didn't want her thinking worse of me.

As I lay in bed that night I thought of Mum and how she always told me to take care. Was I wandering into danger? Maybe, but she would have done the same if she thought it was right. I thought I would never sleep, but I was wrong. It was as if a great weight had been lifted from my mind.

Chapter 6

In a final unexpected blast of winter, the next day brought snow. Great drifts of the stuff, which filled the lanes and fields around the village. It was hard to tell where one thing stopped and another one started – there were no ditches or hedges, just soft gentle folds of pure white, like a never-ending marshmallow lake. The school closed when the electricity lines were so laden with ice they caved in, and the ancient heating system gave up.

In London things hardly ever came to a halt because of snow or, if they did, they were fixed so fast you never really noticed. I guess there were those who hated the inconvenience but, to me, the whole place seemed to take on a magical air. Everyone seemed happy, and went out of their way to help everyone else. We were enchanted by this shiny white world, and in the evenings Dad lit candles and placed them all around the cottage. I challenged him to games of Scrabble or cards, keeping a list of scores pinned to the fireplace.

In the mornings there would be a fresh fall of snow and the village kids would meet at the top of the hill leading down to the church. People found all kinds of objects to use as a make-do sledge, anything they could lay their hands on. Kitchen trays, old pieces of wood or, as in my case, one of Dad's brainwaves – a strong plastic bag filled with coats which, to my surprise, shot down the hill as fast and furious as anything else. I hung on for dear life with M beside me on a bright blue plastic sledge. We only gave up when our coats and boots became too soggy and cold, or our stomachs grumbled for food, whichever came first.

One day when I got back, I found Dad out in the workshop surrounded by bits of wood and rope and lots of tools spread out on the workbench. He'd managed to put together a sledge of sorts and was just finishing it off when I arrived. I was pretty impressed, but more than that, I was pleased to see Dad take an interest in even the smallest of projects again. Since Mum went he'd barely left the house in London, and things hadn't been much different here. I'd hoped he'd take up driving again, but he'd shown no sign and I didn't want to be the first to mention it. I guess I was afraid of how he'd react. Everyone'd said it would take time, so I held my tongue and let him be. I was really chuffed though and I made sure he knew by plastering a great big grin all over my face.

The next morning he came with me to watch his handiwork in action, and before long we were both whizzing down the slope together, tumbling into the snow-laden hedge at the bottom of the hill. It was good for Dad, and good for me too, to see him laughing and enjoying himself. I caught a glimpse of the Dad I used to know and it brought a lump to my throat.

It was during this week that I first went to M's place. I didn't know what to expect, but I should've known … I guess it was the closest thing I'd ever seen to a menagerie. Not only did Pepper race to the gate to welcome me, but a tired old terrier called George raised his head in a half-hearted greeting from where he lay sprawled on the doorstep. He refused to move so we climbed over him. Inside the house a pair of black cats called Big and Small were draped across the mat in front of a Rayburn cooker in the kitchen. I learned that they were mother and daughter.

We wandered down the garden to a large wooden shed, where M proudly introduced me to a rabbit, two hamsters, a tortoise and a pair of white mice, all neatly housed in separate areas with fresh straw and shredded paper. At the far end, the shed had been divided up into sections, each having a small pile of logs, covered in dead leaves and straw.

'This is Mum's,' said M.

'What is it?' I asked, puzzled.

M smiled, 'It's a hedgehog hospital. You won't be

able to see them, they're hibernating.' She must have seen the look of amazement on my face. 'People are always finding injured hedgehogs … they just bring them along to Mum. She'll let these go soon, when the weather warms up. She just loves hedgehogs. We had a whole family of them in the log pile last year, three babies.'

At the bottom of the garden was another small shed, open on one side. As we neared it I heard the rattle of a chain and a small white goat popped its head round the side. M scrambled around in her pocket and brought out a handful of grain and the goat ate them greedily, nuzzling its nose into her pocket for more. She slapped it away playfully. I'd never owned a pet and I envied her as I watched the way they all responded to her.

'How d'you find the time?' I asked.

'It's like having a family,' she explained, 'you just get on with it.'

An idea began to form in the back of my mind. I began to think I'd like a dog myself, but more than that, I had a feeling it might be good for Dad, having an animal to care for. I filed the idea away at the back of my mind along with everything else I wanted to talk to Dad about, whenever the time was right.

Back inside the house, a door I hadn't noticed before opened, and a woman emerged, and with her a whoosh of perfume filled the air. It was so overpowering my nose tingled and I began to sneeze violently. She wore a long striped skirt which swished around her ankles as she walked. Her brown hair was tied up in a knot at the back of her neck and she had the same dark eyes as M.

'Ah, so this must be your Joe then. Has she shown you round the zoo?' she said with a laugh, and I couldn't help noticing a faint blush on M's cheeks as she offered me a tissue from a box on the table.

'It's Mum's little factory in there,' she explained. 'She makes soap ... by hand. She gathers all sorts of stuff – flowers, berries and nettles, honey, even seaweed. Then she adds other things ... like apples or lemons or herbs and flowers. She sells them at the markets or to gift shops. It's mostly tourists who buy them.'

They busied themselves making tea, clattering cups and saucers and rinsing a blackened teapot; I saw the easy way they had with each other. I swallowed hard.

I missed Mum so much sometimes it hurt and right then I longed to feel her arms around me. I turned away, burying my nose in the tissue, and took a deep breath. I had to think of a way to lift Dad out of the sad little world he'd built around himself ... before it was too late.

Chapter 7

By the following weekend the snow was pretty thin on the ground, most of it turned to slush. Just a few icy stretches were left in the shadow of the hedges. It had been a busy week, but my mind had never been far from our meeting with Jasper Barrow.

'Maybe we shouldn't go,' M said, always the sensible one, 'we don't know what we're getting into.'

'I know, I've been thinking the same,' I lied, 'it does seem a bit reckless.' I sighed. 'We should make a plan of some sort, so we can be sure we get back okay.'

'I don't see how we can make a plan when we have no idea what's going to happen on Saturday, or where the old man will take us,' she replied.

'I just have this feeling that it's so ... so vital that we go ... that ...' my voice trailed off lamely and I looked down and studied my feet, not wanting to look at her, not knowing how to say what I wanted to say.

'You're not going to back out are you?' she said. There was a long silence.

'Nope,' I replied, 'I can't, but you are coming with me aren't you?'

''Course I am,' she said with a smile, 'I was just testing you 'cause you were really freaked out the other night.'

On Saturday, just before three, we met in our usual place by the wall. The sun had barely shown its face. It was a dark day, a grey day, so cold and still, as if the day was holding its breath; waiting, like us. We shoved our hands inside our pockets for warmth and headed for the castle walls. This time I went in first.

Jasper Barrow was waiting by the entrance to the dungeons, exactly where we'd seen him that night. My stomach was churning. Had I been letting my imagination run away? What was the old man's secret? He barely spoke, but simply nodded his head and motioned for us to follow him. We slid silently through the arched doorway then made our way inside the largest dungeon. Once again I felt the thick musty air hit the back of my throat.

I was so tense I almost forgot to breathe.

I don't know what I was expecting to see. I flicked my torch around and the feeble light shone dully on the walls. But there was nothing, nothing at all. Then Jasper turned to us. His face looked pinched and white, his eyes deadly serious.

'Listen now,' he began, 'what you're goin' t' see

now, must never be told. *Never*. D'ya understand? 'Tis a wonderful thing ... but 'tis never, *never* to be told!'

His moist old eyes searched our faces, flicking from one to the other, 'You must *swear*, now ... *swear* that this secret will stay between us ... between us three here now.'

I was bursting with questions, but I knew this wasn't the right time to ask them. M caught my eye and gave a slight nod of her head. And that's how we stood, the three of us in a tight little circle as Jasper placed his hands one against the other, as if in prayer. I glanced across at M and followed her lead as I so often did in those days and together we raised our own hands. Jasper began to speak.

'Oh Lord of Legends Great and Good, You have heard my prayers. You have helped me over the years to do my duty, to do my best. It has been my only true purpose in life.' He paused and gently shook his head from side to side. 'But now I am old, the years have caught up with me, like, and the time has come ... the time has come to pass my secret on.'

He held out his hands. 'In these two souls I place my trust completely.'

With these words Jasper reached and took one each of our hands in his. Without knowing why I reached for M's other hand so that all three of us were joined in a circle. 'You must swear now that what is revealed to you today will stay with you two only, in all this world forever?'

My eyes were lowered, but now I lifted them to his and he returned my gaze. Why did he have such trust in me? I didn't understand, but somehow it felt right.

'I … I swear,' my voice echoed round the walls.

'Yes, we will … we swear,' came M's soft reply.

Then Jasper shone his torch up high on the wall, and behind a craggy outcrop of rock I saw a loop of thick chain hanging down. It was attached to an iron ring. Jasper pulled it, using all his strength; then I grasped it too with both hands.

As I did, I heard a loud scraping noise behind me. Turning, I saw a flat rock move from behind us. It swivelled round slowly, grinding against the stone floor, revealing an opening in front of us about four feet high. It was as black as night in there but for a brief moment I imagined there was a dim and distant glow coming from somewhere deep within, and I thought I could hear the faintest tinkle of water. Was this one of my crazy dreams? Was I sleepwalking and in a moment I would wake in my attic room? I looked across at M and wondered if she was thinking the same.

As we entered into a narrow passage a wave of damp air hit my nostrils, and the unmistakable smell of the sea. The passage was about three feet wide with rough reddish rock on either side, cold and shining with trickles of water. I shivered. We began to travel slightly downhill, so I knew we were going even further underground, way beyond the castle itself.

I don't know how far we'd gone before the passageway opened out into a small cave and to my amazement there was a massive door set into the rocks on thick iron hinges. Here Jasper paused, took a long deep breath and looked at us. Once more he told us that we had nothing to fear, and once more my stomach tied itself in knots. The old man produced a key from his pocket and slid it into the lock. It turned with a loud clunk. The door swung back easily with a mighty creaking noise, the echoes bouncing off the rocky walls around us. Jasper laid a hand on my arm, and I felt M's hand sneak inside mine.

Nothing in the world could have prepared me for what was inside. Even my craziest imaginings could not have dreamt it up.

Chapter 8

A blast of warm, smoky air hit us as we stepped inside. Straight away I felt beads of sweat on my forehead. I blinked as my eyes adjusted to the dim light from the candles, which flickered all around the walls of a large room. Well, I say 'room', though it was really a cave, but full of all kinds of stuff, like you'd see in a really old person's house; an ancient bookcase, stacked high with books that looked too big to lift, let alone read; a huge threadbare sofa, its back turned towards us; a patterned rug, frayed and worn from too much wear and tear, the kind I'd seen in stately homes with a sign telling you not to walk on it. An old kettle stood on a small stove in the corner of the room. Who did all this belong to? Jasper lived in his cottage – so who lived here?

M wrinkled her nose, 'I can smell … fireworks?' she whispered.

I nodded. I'd been trying to put a name to the familiar smell too. Suddenly there was a movement from the sofa, and that same snuffling we'd heard in the dungeon, like someone with a heavy cold. Had we disturbed someone? I began to feel uneasy. We shouldn't be here; it was madness.

Instinctively I stepped closer to M. We should never have come.

It suddenly occurred to me then that no one else knew we were here. We had been very foolish and reckless, I should've known better, I should've been more responsible … I should've been looking out for both of us. All this ran through my mind. But it was too late now. We could both be in terrible danger.

Then, the tip of a snout suddenly appeared from round the corner of the sofa and seemed to be sniffing at the air. We both took a step backwards. What the …? If it hadn't been for Jasper I think we would have taken to our heels and run. Gently he propelled us forwards with quiet words of encouragement. Why, I don't know – we barely knew him – but we instinctively trusted him.

The firework smell was stronger now. Then, before I had time to adjust to the gloom, a gleaming, scaly creature uncurled itself and sat upright on the sofa. I heard a gasp from beside me; M's hand was clamped to her mouth. She grabbed my arm to pull me back, but I couldn't move; my legs had deserted me.

The dragon turned its huge head towards us.

Minutes passed.

People talk about time standing still; well, that's exactly what it was like. To this day I can't explain why, but I took a small step forward. With snake-like elegance the creature slithered slowly off the sofa. It stretched its scaly neck causing flickering shades of red and pink to shimmer in the glimmering light of the candles.

The dragon came nearer. It was so close I could have reached out and touched it. It gazed directly at me, its eyes like deep glowing pools drawing me in and I couldn't tear my eyes away. I stared back, like a frightened rabbit, my own tiny image reflected back at me in those huge eyes. The dragon snuffled again and lowered its head towards us, reminding me of M's goat nuzzling for a treat. And all the time I was aware of Jasper watching us, as if he was waiting to see what would happen next.

It was M who finally took a deep breath then stretched out her hand to gently stroke the dragon's head with her finger. Time stood still again, then I reached out too, very, very slowly. I touched its neck, tracing my finger along the slippery scales; they were unexpectedly soft. The dragon turned its gaze on me and flicked out a pointed tongue to touch my wrist. Instinct made me want to pull away, but I held fast, thrilled at the feel of its grainy tongue on my skin. It was an amazing moment. And then we heard a low rumble coming from deep inside the dragon as it gently nuzzled its snout against my chest. Jasper broke the magic.

'Well, blow me,' he chuckled, 'I ain't 'eard 'im do

that, not in a long time. Well I never! Purrs like a bloomin' cat when 'e's 'appy, that 'e does.'

Jasper left us fondling the great creature and went over to the stove in the corner. Before long I was sitting on the sofa with a mug of sweet tea in my still shaky hands. The dragon, aglow with a brilliant crimson colour in the soft light, lay curled at my feet. If I stretched out my toe I could touch the little triangular tip at the end of its tail. M sat on the floor too and drawing an apple from her pocket, she fed small pieces into the dragon's mouth. She had a way with animals that always made me envious; they instinctively seemed to trust her.

My mind was whirling. I could hardly believe that we were sitting drinking tea with one of the world's greatest mythological creatures. And like this we learned Jasper's incredible story.

Jasper settled himself on the edge of the sofa and, wrapping a warm shawl around his knees, he looked at the girl and the dragon and his old eyes shone as he began to talk. Almost all of what Jasper told us that day had been handed down from generation to generation.

Sometime, centuries ago he believed, a young man, a farmhand, had been hunting in the woody scrubland surrounding the castle and had heard the sound of an animal in pain. Thinking he had successfully shot something he hacked his way through the brushy undergrowth. What he saw to his amazement was a young female dragon giving birth to her baby. The mother was so distressed that the brave young man, being used to cows and horses giving birth on the farm, put aside his fear and did what he could to help. The baby dragon was born, but sadly the mother was so weak she died shortly afterwards.

Incredibly, this man had been one of Jasper's ancestors and was so touched by the gentleness of this feared creature that he vowed to care for the young dragon and he brought it home. He and his wife took the creature to a hidden cave down by the shore. They fed and cared for the creature, earning its loyalty and love. They knew that if their secret was discovered the dragon would be slain, for dragons were feared by all. They called him Gerald, after a wise man and a scholar who had been born in the castle in the eleventh century.

At this point Jasper reached forward to touch the dragon's head, fondling its ears. The dragon placed its head affectionately on Jasper's slippered feet, just like a faithful old dog. It was thrilling to see them together.

'See that ol' green book there … on the shelf at the bottom? 'Tis all in there, aye, all there since Gerald was found on the day 'e was born.' Jasper shook his head as if he could hardly believe it himself. I grinned at the funny way Gerald pricked up his ears when he heard his name.

'I swear 'e knows 'is name ... 'e knows what's goin' on that's for sure,' chuckled the old man.

I wandered over to the shelf and knelt on the floor. The book was faded and worn and I was afraid of damaging the fragile pages. It smelt musty, and a cloud of silvery dust raced through the air as I traced my finger over the cover: *'The Keeper's Secret'* it said in faint gold lettering. The care of the dragon had been handed on, its precious secret held safe over hundreds of years as it passed from generation to generation. It was unbelievable that the creature before us was hundreds of years old. It was the stuff of dreams, but the living proof was lying at our feet.

Jasper rubbed his chin. He was remembering the moment his own parents revealed their secret to him. He was nine years old and his mother had taken him down into the dungeon where his father waited. He said he had always felt there was some mystery, something missing from his life until that moment. From then on he had had only one purpose. I wondered how old Jasper was too.

Jasper's face suddenly saddened and he told us how his greatest worry over the years was that he had had no child of his own to be the next keeper of the secret. He had never married, and as time went on he had worried who would take over his role. He spent many nights lying awake, fretting; all his life he had kept himself away from people for fear of discovery. There was nobody he could trust.

He turned towards me, 'Then one night, not so long ago, I 'ad a dream. I saw a young boy sailin' a tall ship in the bay. There was a bad storm goin' on and the boy was alone. Suddenly, I 'eard something … Gerald wailin' through the wind, callin' to the boy. I woke up suddenly and I knowed straight away it was a sign … all I 'ad to do was wait.'

I turned towards him in amazement.

'I … I had that dream … more than once,' I spoke slowly, hardly able to believe what I had just heard. 'It was exactly like that. I was … on the ship, the wind was howling, the sails were flapping and slapping, and the noise … I … I was losing control. I was frightened. Then I heard a sad wailing. It seemed so real, so close, as if it was calling me, trying to tell me something … I couldn't shake it off … the feeling that something was terribly wrong, but I didn't understand … I felt there was a message in the dream … meant for me, and …' my voice trailed off self-consciously,

'Aye, aye, I knew 'twas you soon as I laid eyes on you t'other night. 'Tis meant to be boy,' said Jasper.

M was watching us from her place on the rug, her hand on Gerald's neck, and I knew she was wondering why I hadn't told her about the dream.

'Was I in the dream?' she asked, quietly. 'I mean ... whichever ... dream ...' Her voice trailed off.

'N ... no,' I stammered, 'but I woke up really suddenly. I guess I didn't get to the part with you in it.' Her face broke slowly into a smile.

'Yeah, right,' she grinned.

We spent the rest of the afternoon listening to Jasper's stories. There had been times when he had feared discovery. The village was not as quiet as it used to be. There were many more houses now and more people. The area had always been popular with holidaymakers and was getting busier every year. It was becoming harder and harder to keep Gerald hidden; he had had to spend more and more time cooped up in the cave. And, sighed Jasper, Gerald loved company. But he was, most likely, the last of his kind. He shook his head sadly.

As the afternoon drew to a close Jasper took us through another narrow opening at the far end of the cave, where the passageway went on. It was even steeper now, sloping downwards as we moved along in single file, Jasper and Gerald leading while M and I followed, our torches throwing shadowy shapes against the rocks. Soon I could taste salt in my mouth and I heard the sound of waves crashing on the shore. Jasper ordered us to switch our torches off. He went forward alone before beckoning us to follow, his finger raised to his lips. We emerged into a tiny shingle cove, far round the corner from the main beach. The sea lapped at the craggy rocks surrounding the cove. Gerald waited in the mouth of the cave, his head held high, looking out to sea. It was almost dark now, for we had been in the castle for hours. Once Jasper was sure that there was no one else around Gerald made his way across the shingle and swam out into the water. I don't know why I was so surprised. Tales of dragons showed pictures of them flying and breathing fire, so I had never thought that a dragon would swim. Jasper noticed our astonished looks. He told us that he had never seen Gerald fly, that it was too dangerous to even try it; he would be sure to be spotted.

He had often wondered himself if Gerald could fly. But many years ago, he had realised that Gerald was sickening for something, and that he had no way of really getting the exercise a dragon needed to keep him healthy and strong. He was worried; he had noticed Gerald going off his food. So one summer night he brought him down to the bay and gently persuaded him into the water. They had frolicked amongst the waves, swimming far out to sea, and it was clear that the dragon was enjoying himself. Since then it had become almost a nightly ritual. Even in the winter months Gerald would often take a dip in the sea, while Jasper watched from the little cove.

I will always remember that first day, watching as Gerald's gleaming body curled and dived through the deep, almost black water, cutting through it in shafts of brilliant red and purple. M and I sat on the rocks in companionable silence. There was no need for words. We were completely enthralled by this beautiful creature. We knew our whole lives had changed from that day onwards, our futures mapped out for us, and we resolved to keep this secret safe no matter what.

But that was just the beginning; little did we know what would happen next.

Chapter 9

For the next few months we lived an almost idyllic existence. It seemed as if life would always be like this. Our world revolved around Gerald and he began to trust us. Almost every day brought some new discovery. One balmy summer night we built a small fire in the little cove and were delighted when Gerald puffed out his cheeks and blew a flicker of flame to light it. We cooked beans and sausages and offered them to him, but like a child he viewed them with disgust. We toasted slices of bread on sticks over the flames and watched in amusement as he devoured slice after slice, the thick, melted butter dripping from his chin. We were thrilled with our new responsibilities, spending as much time with him as we could spare between school and home.

We spent long hours in Jasper's vegetable patch where he showed us all the delicious leaves and vegetables Gerald liked best – huge dark green cabbages, leafy spinach and bright bunches of carrots. We listened carefully, making notes, knowing that some day it would be up to us to provide enough food for Gerald. Jasper took us into the woods and showed us where to find wild garlic, nettles and lush grass, which he also used to supplement Gerald's diet. It wasn't always possible to take him out to graze on the woodland plants, he explained, sometimes it was just too risky.

There were times, especially when I was lying in bed at night, that I wished I could tell Dad all about it. I knew he could be trusted and would've helped, but we'd given our solemn promise to Jasper and I couldn't go back on it, no matter what. It meant I often had to make excuses, but Dad was still so preoccupied in his own sad world that he never questioned anything I did or anywhere I went. Maybe he was just glad to see me getting on with my life in a way he couldn't seem to. I wished I could help him more, but by then I had no idea how to reach him. We were miles apart and I didn't know how to make it right.

*

We'd just broken up for the summer holidays when something happened which shattered this peaceful existence. I was sitting on the floor in the cottage, a bowl of water in front of me, trying to find a puncture in my bike tyre. It had happened on the way home from Jasper's; I'd had to push the bike the rest of the way home and I wanted to fix it ready for the next day. I knew Dad would help if I asked him, but I thought I ought to at least try and do it myself first. I wasn't really paying attention to the TV in the corner of the room. Dad was listening to some news report about dairy farmers. Then the reporter changed stories ...

> *'There have been several reported sightings of an unidentified creature swimming off the North Pembrokeshire coast today, near the lifeboat station at St. Justinian. The Coastguard has received at least twenty calls in the course of the afternoon. The animal reportedly has a long spiked tail, a greenish pink body and a long neck. One woman described it as "dragonlike". Many believe it to be a hoax, since the description bears a close resemblance to similar reported sightings of the legendary Loch Ness monster. But, hoax or not, one local caught this image on camera ...'*

I dropped the tyre, splashing water on to the floor, and had to stop myself crying out. Dad noticed my reaction and shifted over on the sofa to make room for me. Slowly I sat down with a heavy plop beside him. I couldn't believe what I was seeing. It was a bad picture, cloudy, grey and spotted with drops of water, as if it had been taken from a boat. But, there was no doubt about it. There was Gerald! And yet it wasn't; we'd been with him all afternoon. Slowly it dawned on me ... if it wasn't Gerald ... then ...

I wanted to hear more, but the newsreader switched to something about traffic congestion on the M4 and I sat in a daze, my thoughts whirling madly round and round. Dad looked at me.

He laughed, 'Someone's idea of a joke I suppose.' And he shrugged his shoulders and turned his attention back to the rest of the news.

'Yeah, most likely,' I nodded, and smiled weakly, too stunned to say more, then quickly busied myself with the tyre, hiding my face from Dad in case he guessed something was up. It was one of the longest nights of my life. It was getting late. I couldn't go out again, and since Dad stayed in the room the whole time I had no chance to make a quick call to M. I just had to curb my impatience and wait till morning.

I couldn't sleep. The night was hot and muggy. I stood at my window, staring towards the sea, wrestling with crazy thoughts. Could there be another dragon out there? We'd all just assumed Gerald was the only one, but why? Why shouldn't there be another one? And not that far away either! I spent a long restless night tossing and turning in my bed. In the end I put the light on and took down a history book with a chapter on dragon-lore, and pored over it till the early hours when I fell into another of my troubled dreams.

Chapter 10

The next day it was headline news. People were convinced there was some truth to the sightings. My heart sank as I watched the TV reports. They'd wasted no time. Newspaper reporters and TV crews were already camped out on the cliff tops and the surrounding fields at St. Justinian. There had been another sighting, close to shore. It was only a matter of time before the creature was caught. A National Park Warden was interviewed and said that it was all a hoax, a mistake; they'd scoured the area themselves, but had seen nothing. A local farmer was interviewed; he had been out with binoculars at first light and he'd seen a shadowy shape, with a long tail, diving below the surface. He was convinced it was real.

I felt sick. Imagine if it had been Gerald! I switched the TV off, I couldn't watch any longer. The poor creature, hunted down, getting hungry and too frightened to go ashore; but it would have to come ashore sooner or later.

Unable to face breakfast I threw a jumper on and left before Dad got up. I didn't want to face him or make excuses today. I headed down the hill and at the village shop I bought a copy of all the newspapers on sale. I sank down on the path leading to the castle and hoped M would show up. It wasn't long before she spotted me. One look at her face told me she'd heard the news too. With barely a word we hurried on to Jasper's cottage, where we found him waiting for us. He was listening to the latest news on the radio and he held his finger to his lips as we approached. He shook his head in disbelief as we listened to a woman being interviewed. It was the same one who'd said it was a *'dragonlike'* creature. She said she feared for the safety of her children. She wanted something done about it.

We sat round in Jasper's small kitchen, each slumped over a newspaper trying to glean the facts as best we could. By lunchtime there was more news, and we listened in dismay ...

'Following reported sightings of a dragonlike creature off the North Pembrokeshire coast, the army has been drafted in to help with the search for the creature, which could be dangerous. Local residents are concerned for their safety, and farmers are worried about their livestock. A special taskforce has been set up just outside the tiny lifeboat station at St. Justinian, and the area is swarming with reporters and onlookers hoping to catch a glimpse of the elusive creature. One local

hotelier said business had never been so good.
We'll keep you updated as this story develops.'

Later we went to see Gerald and sat huddled together on the old sofa ... somehow we had to think of something. By late afternoon we'd worked out a kind of plan. It was pretty ambitious, and Gerald would play a major part. We worked on the assumption that the dragon would be friendly like Gerald, but we knew this was risky, and we all agreed that we wouldn't risk either our own lives or Gerald's if things turned out differently. We would back off if we thought anything bad was going to happen. It was dangerous, reckless, but we had to try; this was Gerald's only chance of finding a companion. We just had to take it.

We went over and over the details making sure we hadn't overlooked anything. I wondered how much Gerald understood as he pricked up his ears and seemed to pay attention to everything we said. We couldn't do it without him and I knew he wouldn't let us down.

The first thing I had to do was convince Dad. I hated lying to him, but this time I had no choice. I invented an invitation to go on a camping trip with one of the boys from school, a few days just a mile or so away, a chance to try our skills at setting up a tent and campfire cooking. In the end it was easy, and I felt guilty, Dad thought it was a great idea for the start of the holidays. I wondered if he was glad to get me out from under his feet. We'd made no plans for the holidays ourselves: summer was halfway gone, and as yet we hadn't even tried out the kayak. I'd been going to suggest it, but the moment never seemed quite right and I didn't want to put Dad on the spot.

He didn't seem to notice what I did these days. Don't get me wrong, I knew he cared about me, he was always there if I needed him, but I got the distinct impression he would rather be alone. As time went on he'd become more and more reclusive, locked away in his own little world. In a flash it suddenly dawned on me that Dad needed help, something or someone to shake him out of this in a way that I couldn't. I made up my mind to do something about it as soon as the dragon-rescue was over. I resolved to get M to help me sort Dad out once and for all. If anyone knew what to do she would.

Chapter 11

It was one of those wild nights when all you can hear is the wind in the trees and the rain bouncing off the ground in sharp bursts. It was turning dark as we set off for the bay. A storm was building; there would be gale force winds before the night was over. I looked round at M as she struggled against the wind. Her hair was stuck to her face; she looked sick with fear. I knew she didn't want me to go in weather like this, but this was a perfect night for it: there would be no one out tonight. I grabbed her arm and we hurried down to the shore. The tide was in, just a few yards from the mouth of the cave. I was warm in spite of the weather, and my wetsuit felt strange under my jacket.

They were waiting just inside the cave; Jasper looking worried and perhaps I should've been too. But I had Gerald. He would get me to St. Justinian in the only way he knew how. By swimming. I trusted him completely. He lay down flat on the sand and I climbed onto his broad scaly neck. Earlier on I'd taken the plastic waterproof box from the kayak and stuffed a change of clothes, a kagoule, my watch and a pair of canvas shoes inside, as well as two packets of biscuits, some sandwiches, four apples and a small bottle of water. At the last minute I'd added a small radio, a five-pound note and some loose change. I'd hidden the box inside my rucksack, which Jasper now secured tightly to my back. Then he took a piece of strong rope and made a sort of bridle round Gerald's neck, looping it tightly around my body, leaving enough spare to make a loop which I could hold on to. M looked out at the sky and the swirling wind. I was surprised when she reached up and gave me a quick hug.

'I wish I was going with you,' she said.

I shook my head, 'I know, but you have to stay and help Jasper, you've a much more important job to do here.' Their role was crucial; they were to build a decoy and it would need to be a good one – a lifelike image of a dragon which they would float out to sea. This would draw the crowds away from St. Justinian where I was heading in my search.

I turned to Jasper, 'Give me two nights … then … just go ahead … don't wait. It's our only chance. I'll try and make contact, as soon as I can find a phone box.' The old man nodded gravely then grasped my hand in both of his.

'God be with you both,' he said, and he ran his hands over Gerald's scaly back as if it might be for the last time. I looked away; I couldn't bear to think how I would feel if anything happened to Gerald.

I looked up at the sky and the boiling sea beneath it. There was a glimpse of silvery moonlight but no sooner did it appear than it was hidden behind the angry clouds which scudded across its face. The sea looked equally angry. The waves had whipped themselves into a frenzy; it was as if the sea and the sky had waged a war against each other and Gerald and I were about to head right into the middle of it.

Gerald raised himself gently. Sitting on his back I felt like a Bedouin in the desert, or Lawrence of Arabia. I strapped my mask and snorkel around my neck, ready for when I might need them. As Gerald waded into the waves I turned and looked back at M, standing on a small rock, her hair blown back from her face. She raised her hand and I waved, wanting to reach out and take her with me.

It didn't feel right leaving her behind, but I had to. If our plan was to work, she and Jasper had their work cut out and I knew they would do everything in their power to fulfil their task. Their job was crucial; they were to build a decoy and it would need to be a good one; a lifelike image of a dragon which they would float out to sea. This would draw the crowds away from St.Justinian where I was heading in my search.

I was glad to be so far above the water, but it soon crept inside my wetsuit in an ice-cold slick. Before long the water was up to Gerald's neck. The waves crashed past us one after the other and I clung on for dear life. It seemed as if I would be swept away at any minute. Time after time I was drenched in spray as wave after wave broke over us, on and on they came with barely a break in between. But Gerald never faltered, he swam strong and true and soon we were out beyond the headland and rounding the corner. I wanted to look back. I knew M would still be watching, but I doubt I could have seen her. Then, the tiny bay was far behind and we were out in the open sea.

The water rose up in massive swells, towering above our heads before collapsing into huge gaping holes. I held on tight. I remembered my dream; this was exactly what it had been like. Everything had been leading up to this. Gerald swam through the storm that night and the wind howled all around us until I thought it would never stop. He used his wings like flippers, ploughing through the water with ease. But there were moments when I thought we might not make it, that I might be swept into the waves and lose sight of Gerald altogether. I thanked God for the rope, which held me fast. Although I struggled to stay focused it was difficult; I soon became tired.

Once I imagined I saw Mum between the dancing waves; she was standing in a dip in the sea, watching me, watching over me, and that gave me

courage. Her familiar words echoed in my ears ...
*'You can achieve anything if you really try. If you want
something you have to strive for it. Anything's possible
if you give it your best shot.'* She always encouraged
me in whatever I did, and I knew she would now,
no matter how foolish and dangerous it might be. I
wondered if I really took after her. Dad was the quiet
sensible one, thinking things through before he
made a decision; was I more like Mum, reckless and
impulsive? She was so brave; could I ever be really
like her? I felt guilty for deceiving Dad though, for
putting myself in danger. I was all he had left. I had
to get back safely.

We crossed the busy shipping lanes at the mouth
of the haven, steering clear of the oil tankers, moored
now to weather the storm, and I thanked God for
the wild night, the cloudy sky and the heaving
sea, which helped keep us hidden. We passed a
lighthouse set high on the headland, throwing its
eerie arc of light into the storm. Gerald steered us
clear, I had no need to guide him: he instinctively
seemed to know when there was danger. I glimpsed
a distant light and I hoped this was the lighthouse
at Skokholm Island, one of a group of island bird
sanctuaries just off the mainland. I'd spent hours
studying the map, it was imprinted on my brain,
and I carried one in my bag, inside the plastic box,
in case we should need it.

The islands loomed out of the storm suddenly like the shadows of misshapen giants. As we approached, the sea sucked and slapped at the rocks surrounding them. It sounded dead creepy in the dark. We must have travelled around thirty miles. It was time to rest. My face was cold and my nose and mouth stung from the salt which had dried on them.

We headed towards Grassholm, the smaller of the islands and the furthest from the mainland; from there it was due north to Ramsey Island and St. Justinian. It was almost dawn. At last the wind began to drop. In the distance the sun was just peeping its head above the horizon; the sky was streaked with pink. It held the promise of a good day, as if the storm had washed everything clean and tidied it all up. I couldn't help thinking that it was a good omen; that my madcap race across a raging sea would not be in vain after all.

We made our way into a tiny deserted cove. Gerald hauled himself from the sea and flopped down on the dry sand. I patted and hugged him, made a big fuss of him. He was exhausted, and I loved him for his courage and strength. I had never doubted he would get us here.

A small thin stream of water trickled down the side of the rocks; I cupped my hands together to rinse the salt from my face and I tasted its sweet freshness on my salty lips. Gerald lapped at it with his grainy tongue until his thirst was quenched. I was hungry too, but we were too tired to eat. I spread my jacket and wetsuit on a rock and hoped the breeze would dry them out. It felt good to be in dry clothes again. We found a large craggy outcrop of rock on a grassy slope above the bay, large enough to give us some shelter and hide us from view. I lay down there with my back against the rocks and Gerald lay in front of me, shielding me from the cool breeze. I wished I could tell M that we had made it this far. I felt warm and safe and soon fell asleep. So far, so good.

Chapter 12

I woke to the sound of Gerald lapping at a trickling stream. I shook myself awake and reached for my bag and found my watch. It was gone two in the afternoon; we'd slept for hours. I ventured out from under the rock and walked slowly down to the sea, looking around carefully and listening for any unusual sounds. All was well, just the gentle sound of the sea lapping the shore and the occasional gull shrieking overhead. The wind had almost disappeared, leaving just a warm gentle breeze. If it stayed like this then the last leg of our journey would be easier.

We were on the far side of the island, out of sight of anyone on the mainland. Our only danger as far as I could see was from boats, which might venture close. I kept watch, sitting on a rock above the sea, while Gerald grazed on small grasses and flowers at the edge of the cliff. I was ravenous and I wolfed down the sandwiches, saving some for later. Then I shared the apples with Gerald, holding them out flat on the palm of my hand the way M did. She was never far from my thoughts. I wished I could be there to see how their end of the plan was working out. I had slept like a log, but I doubted she had slept at all.

The afternoon drew on; we had several hours to kill before it would be safe to leave. Suddenly Gerald stopped grazing and pricked up his ears. And then I heard it too. An engine. I jumped off the rock and hid behind it, just a few seconds before a large yellow dinghy rounded the corner into the cove. Gerald had crouched down as best he could amongst a group of reddish coloured rocks, the sea lapping gently against them. From where I was, I could still see his back end sticking out though. The rocks just weren't quite big enough to hide him completely.

There were two men in the dinghy. As they pulled into the shallows and climbed out I could see by their jackets that they worked for the National Park. I watched from my hiding place as they took several plastic bottles from the boat. They were wearing long yellow rubber boots almost up to the tops of their legs. They busied themselves collecting water samples from near the rocks, chatting amongst themselves as they wandered nearer and nearer towards Gerald.

I could barely breathe. I tried desperately to think of something to distract them. They began to pull at a tangle of fishing net lying amongst the rocks, which I guessed might harm sea birds or other marine life which thrived on the island. They were getting closer and closer to Gerald as they struggled with the net. I had no choice.

As casually as I could I sauntered out onto the sand. The men were startled to see me, a lone boy in a deserted cove. But I was getting good at making up stories; I'd had plenty of practice lately.

'Hello, why are you collecting the sea-water?' I asked, sounding as interested as I could manage, but painfully aware of my heart thumping so loudly against my rib-cage they were bound to hear it.

'Good God!' said the tall one, spinning round at the sound of my voice, 'where on earth did you spring from?'

'You on your own lad?' asked the other one, rubbing a bearded chin and looking around.

'Oh, Mum's walking up ... there somewhere,' I pointed vaguely towards the cliff top. 'Er ... she's ... a photographer. She loves looking at all the flowers round here.' I secretly congratulated myself on my inventiveness. 'She's not far away. She'll be down soon.'

'How the ... how d'you get here?' asked the tall one again.

'Uh? Oh, my Dad ...' I did my best to sound convincing, '... Dad's boat. He's fishing, round the corner there.' I pointed away from Gerald and at last they turned their backs on him. I glanced at my watch. 'He should be back soon. I stayed here … to explore … the, umm … rock pools. There's loads of starfish … over there.' Again I pointed away from Gerald. I was starting to blabber; I was trying too hard. I took a deep breath and tried to relax.

The men looked concerned. I guess it was their job to make sure that people were safe, as well as the wildlife. I stuffed my hands into my pockets and pushed my toes into the sand. I wanted them to pack up and go, but they didn't look convinced.

'Look, what's your name sonny?' said the one with the beard.

'Uh, Ben,' I lied.

'It's not safe wandering round on your own in a place like this. Wait here, I'll climb up and see if I can find your Mum.' He headed up towards the cliff top, leaving the other man with me. He began to pack the plastic bottles back in the dinghy. That at least was a hopeful sign, but somehow I didn't think they'd go and leave me here on my own, not with dusk just an hour away.

'I think I'll climb round the corner, see if I can see Dad,' I said, 'I hope he's okay. He should've been back by now. He tends to lose track of time when he's fishing.' I tried to sound worried.

'Look,' said the tall man, 'you wait here Ben, I'm gonna take the boat round, see if I can see your Dad. What's he got … a dinghy?'

'Erm … yeah, it's orange,' I said, 'should be easy to spot.'

I watched as he started up the engine and sped away from the cove. He was out of sight in seconds. I glanced up at the cliffs to make the sure the other man had disappeared from sight. There was no sign of him; he was busy looking for my imaginary mother. We were on our own again. I didn't waste time.

I dashed back to the rock and chucked my things into the plastic box, throwing my wetsuit on as fast as I could. There was no time to think about the rope now, I would have to manage without it; the sea was much calmer and every second we stayed on this beach was a second nearer disaster. I put on my mask and snorkel and Gerald and I submerged ourselves under the water as fast as we could. I could already hear the hum of the dinghy returning. I wondered how long they would spend looking for me. I smiled to myself … the last place they would think to look would be out at sea.

Pretty soon it was dark enough to stay on the surface. I lay flat on Gerald's back, stretching my arms around his spiny neck and like that we headed due north.

Chapter 13

It was a clear, calm summer's night; the wind had died down completely. We made good time, the sea was almost flat now, just a gentle swell rising and falling. The moon was bright, making a broad yellow band on the shimmering surface of the water, but we kept clear of the coastline. I felt more exposed; I knew we could be easily spotted on a night like this. Gerald kept his head down, raising it just slightly out of the water so he could breathe. The gentle movement of the sea almost lulled me to sleep.

Eventually we approached Ramsey Island, which rose from the sea like a sleeping monster, flat, but for two humplike hills on its back. And then I saw them – hundreds of lights up on the mainland overlooking the sea. Camping lights, lanterns, firelight. My stomach lurched. I caught a whiff of smoke and barbecued meat, and in dismay realized I was looking at a great mass of tents and caravans. It was as if the whole world had descended on this one small area.

Gerald guided us round towards the back of the island. We were still a good way off when suddenly I heard a loud engine noise. At first I couldn't tell where it was coming from. I froze in horror as a searchlight beam sped across the water towards us and I suddenly realized that it was coming from above, on its own mission to seek out the mysterious creature of the sea. But Gerald was way ahead of me. With a flick of his tail he took us safely beneath the surface. I grappled for my snorkel, balancing myself lower down on his neck so that the snorkel's tip just broke the water's surface. When all was quiet and safe again we made a dash for the safety of a solitary rocky outcrop and, finding a tiny sliver of silvery sand on which to rest, we pressed ourselves as close against the rocks as we could. It was all we could do and I just hoped we were hidden from view. I quickly changed back into my dry clothes, but I stayed cold and shivering till dawn, when the first rays of sun began to warm our weary bodies.

It was too dangerous for Gerald to forage for food. I didn't think it was safe to go nearer to the island. So, while I wolfed down the rest of the sandwiches, Gerald made short work of a whole packet of biscuits and the last apple. I longed for a drink of hot sweet tea but had to make do with the last of the water, most of which I managed to trickle onto Gerald's salty tongue. I knew this was the most dangerous time for us. We had already heard engine noises and realized that the search had been renewed at first light.

But if our plan was going to work, and if M and Jasper had succeeded in their part in the plan, things were about to change.

At nine o'clock I turned on the little radio, keeping the volume as low as I could.

'The search for the elusive dragonlike creature off the Welsh coast has moved further south. At 4.30 this morning a farmer reported seeing the creature in the water near Caldey Island in South Pembrokeshire, close to the popular seaside town of Tenby. Since then there have been several more sightings in the area. Until today, all sightings have been in the vicinity of St. Justinian in North Pembrokeshire. However, the description given by the farmer is almost identical … a long pointed tail and horse-like head. On Tuesday the army were drafted in to help locate the animal, but to date have been unsuccessful. Reports are coming in that the soldiers, along with television and radio reporters and members of the public, who had descended on the area surrounding St. Justinian, have de-camped and are making their way south. This has caused considerable congestion on main routes into Tenby, which is already busy with summer holidaymakers. Members of the public are being advised to avoid the area. We'll keep you updated as more news comes in.'

I almost whooped for joy. Our plan had worked. Jasper and M had done it! I hugged Gerald and he must have wondered what all the fuss was about. Now all we had to do was stay low and try to find the dragon ourselves.

I took out the little map and studied it again, taking my bearings for St. Justinian. The little lifeboat station was almost directly opposite from where we were. We waited another hour before edging our way out from the rocks and slipping into the cool water once again. We gave the island a wide berth. Lying along Gerald's back, almost totally submerged, I risked a glance at the mainland. I smiled as I watched a long line of cars and vans heading away southwards, all their belongings packed inside, but I knew that just one slip from us could bring the whole lot of them back here again. Time was precious – how long did we have?

I caught a flash of red and recognized the painted tin roof of St. Justinian's lifeboat station from a picture in one of Dad's books. We were so close now. This was more or less exactly where the dragon had been seen. We swam past and turned inland, searching the coastline for a safe landing place.

Once again we found a small gravelly cove, so tiny that Gerald almost filled up the entire space. I climbed up the shoreline as high as I could and sat on a rock. I scanned the water. And then the enormity of our situation hit me. I realized how useless this journey might be after everything we'd done. Hundreds of people had been searching for the dragon for days. They'd had all sorts of equipment – helicopters, cameras, binoculars and goodness knows what else. If the army couldn't find it, what made me think I could? I was just a useless boy.

My heart sank.

We moved on, slightly further north, then stopped and searched again. We re-traced our steps, going over and over the same length of coastline where the dragon had been spotted. But it was no use, there was nothing. Were we too late? The poor thing might have drowned by now. But I refused to give up hope, not now that we'd come this far. The afternoon drew on and I felt more and more desperate. If we couldn't find the dragon then we would simply have to go back; that much I had promised Jasper. I felt sad and alone.

We'd been searching for what seemed like hours, up and down the same stretch of coast near the lifeboat station, and were just resting on a small grassy bank beneath some rocks. Suddenly Gerald started acting strangely. His ears pricked up, and he began to swing his tail back and fore. I had never seen him do that before. He stood right at the water's edge, his head on one side, stepping from one foot to the other in a funny sort of dance, his tail slowly swaying. I watched him from my spot on the rocks. Then he turned and looked back at me and I watched in horror as he moved off into the water, leaving me stranded on the rocks. I called him, but he took no notice. He was hell bent on something I didn't understand. I kept one eye on the top of his head gliding silently through the water, while I scrambled across the rocks, trying to keep sight of him. It was hard going and I could hardly keep up.

Finally I stopped, unable to believe that Gerald was leaving me behind. I stood gaping with horror as he disappeared completely from sight.

Chapter 14

I clambered over the rocks in a blind panic, my heart thumping, not caring that I was scraping my arms and legs over and over until they bled. About twenty minutes later I spotted him and thanked heaven as he turned for the shore. And then I heard something, a distant sort of snuffly, whining noise. I realized it was coming from Gerald. He had stopped swimming and was staring intently at the shoreline. I hurried on, cursing each boulder I had to climb over or clamber round, making small detours as I negotiated my way, all the time fearing I would lose sight of him again. But he hadn't moved.

From my perch I watched as Gerald swam slowly towards a narrow opening. He pulled himself from the water. I watched as he moved forward, pushing his way between the rocks, which lined the shore. I was way above him now looking down, but still a good way off. A few minutes later I lost sight of him again. I looked for a way down, and had to retrace my steps before I could find one. At long last I jumped down onto the shingle, landing awkwardly on my knees. As I rounded the corner I saw the entrance to a narrow cave in front of me, and knew that was where Gerald had gone. I called him softly, but my instincts told me to stay where I was, so I waited and watched. I hadn't lost my trust in him; how could I? He had brought me this far. He was in there somewhere and would come when he was ready.

I lost track of time, waiting, wondering whether to follow him into the cave. Then I heard a noise and Gerald's head emerged from the mouth of the cave. I felt tears prickle my eyes; my worst fear was that we would lose each other. We had to keep each other safe, even if it meant we didn't bring back the other dragon. He shuffled towards me, almost sheepishly, and I reached out and stroked his face, glad to see him back safe and sound. But then he began to move backwards, and I heard a noise from behind him.

A dragon limped slowly across the sand towards us. It was smaller than Gerald, but just as beautiful. Its delicate pinks and greens glimmered in the light. The dragon stretched its slender neck several times, as if it had been cramped up for a long time. The bright sun reflected off a sea-green scaly back, and rippled across a pale pink belly. I kept completely still, but I felt as if my bones had turned to jelly.

Suddenly the dragon saw me and began to back away towards the cave again, arching its neck, its lips turned into a snarl as it hissed and lowered its head as if it might charge at me. I noticed thin trickles of smoke coming from its nostrils. To this day I don't know why I didn't run. I guess something stuck in my head about standing your ground if confronted by a wild animal; that running's the last thing you should do. Gerald turned his head and nuzzled the dragon's neck, which seemed to calm it down. It struck me then how thin and weak it looked. Compared to Gerald the poor thing looked decidedly unhealthy.

I took a few slow steps backwards. I didn't want to alarm it again; there was no telling what might happen. Being careful not to make any sudden movements I swung the bag from my back and took out the last of the biscuits, holding a couple out on the flat of my hand. The dragon watched as Gerald ate them greedily. I placed another one on my hand and held it out. But the other dragon refused to come any closer, so I took a small step forward, glad that Gerald was close by. I knew he wouldn't let anything happen to me. The dragon craned its neck towards me until it touched my outstretched hand. It licked at the biscuit nervously but left it there, and I suddenly realized something was wrong. It wasn't just thin; this dragon was ill. Then it turned round and began to lick at its tail, and that's when I saw it.

A huge great gash almost slicing the tail in two. My heart sank. With a wound like that, this dragon would never be able to swim back with us.

*

I hated leaving them, but I had no choice. I had to get help. If all the reporters and the army came back, we'd never get out of here. Gerald nuzzled against my chest then gave me a little push as if he understood I had to go. The two dragons went back inside the cave. I prayed they would be safe in there till I got back, but they had no food and just a trickle of water running down the wall of the cave. The injured dragon was getting weaker every minute. I searched the headland for a way to climb up to the coast path, but it was really tricky.

When we moved to Wales Dad had told me to be sensible around the cliffs, to stick to the paths, not to wander away from them. There were always fresh rock falls, which showed how precarious these cliffs were. It was hard not to rush though, looking for solid footholds, testing great handfuls of spiky grasses, before grasping hold of them and pulling myself up a little bit further. It was slow going; the sun beat down, baking the rocks around me. Sweat soaked my shirt and trickled down my face. I heaved a sigh of relief when I finally reached a grassy knoll and rolled over onto the path.

I looked left and then right, clueless as to which way to turn. I wished I had the little map with me, but in my haste I realized I'd left everything behind in the rucksack. I knew Whitesands Bay was further north around the corner, but I couldn't remember how far it was. It was a large stretch of sand popular with surfers; there'd be a phone box there, surely. I knew roughly where St. Justinian was too, but I couldn't see the little lifeboat station from where I was now; it could be even further. In my mad dash to keep up with Gerald I'd lost track of how far we'd travelled. I could have kicked myself. I should have made a point of finding out where the public phone boxes were. I glanced at my watch. It was gone two. Getting late. One way or another we needed to get away from here today. We couldn't risk staying any longer. Without wasting another second I turned north and prayed it was a good choice.

First of all, in spite of the heat I kept up a steady jog. The path was deserted. The sky was a deep, cloudless blue, with no let up from the sun's glare. I felt my face burning and my throat was so dry it hurt to swallow. I wished I'd filled up the plastic bottle from the trickle inside the cave, but in my haste, I hadn't even given it a thought. I tried to stay focused. Tried not to think about the injured dragon ... and Gerald ... what if Gerald ... I almost turned back. The thought of anything happening to Gerald was unbearable.

My anxiety added to the heat, and before long my head was thumping and I had trouble focusing. I stumbled along, racking my ankles, scraping my arms and legs against the thorny golden gorse at the sides of the path. Its perfume rose in clouds and filled my nostrils. Overpowering and sickly sweet, it made my empty stomach churn. My headache got worse and in spite of the heat I began to shiver. I wanted to lie down for a moment, but I daren't. There was no shelter here, and I was afraid I would fall asleep in the heat of the sun. I wondered how much further away Whitesands was. With each curve of the path I hoped it was the last, but there was always another, and then another. I began to wonder if I should turn inland and try to find a house with a phone. Without thinking properly, I left the path, climbed over a fence and dropped down into a field.

I began to run again, blindly, scarcely lifting my eyes, following the edge of the field, barely conscious of my surroundings. Then suddenly I tripped on something and found myself flying through the air before falling headlong into the hedge, hitting my head on the stump of a tree and rolling onto the grass. I lay there for several minutes, blissfully aware of soft grass beneath my head and then I closed my eyes.

Chapter 15

I don't know how long I slept or how long the noise had been hovering on the edge of my brain, but suddenly I registered the gentle hum of an engine. I stood up too quickly, which made me feel dizzy and sick again. My mouth was so dry I could barely swallow. I looked anxiously at the sky, expecting to see another helicopter. But there was nothing, just clear blue sky and the sun beating down. I looked around puzzled; then I realized the noise was coming from beyond the hedge. I sprang up and fought my way into the bushes, climbing my way through till I found a piece of old wooden fence. I clambered up until I could see over the top.

There was a big field in front of me dotted with little rectangular bales of hay spilling out from a machine being pulled along slowly by an ancient looking tractor. The bales lay in straight lines up and down the field like boxes, while some were stacked in small piles. Another tractor was droning along at snail's pace, while two men, using long-handled forks, swung the bales up onto a trailer, one on each side, and another man stood on the moving trailer stacking them tightly together. I watched for a few moments, weighing up the odds. Should I keep away from them, even though I desperately needed help? I weighed up the risks; I couldn't help thinking there must be a farmhouse nearby.

As I stood watching, a woman entered the field with a basket on her arm. The men let out whoops of joy, then the tractors stopped, and they all trudged over towards the woman. They sat around on bales of hay, or on the ground. I watched them for a few moments, still hesitating, but it was the sight of a large metal can, which she produced from the basket, that helped me make up my mind.

I climbed awkwardly over the hedge, scratching my arms and legs even more and limped weakly across the field towards them.

'Hey,' I shouted across 'excuse me ... erm, is there a phone near here?' Five pairs of eyes looked up in surprise.

'What's up, sonny?' asked a big burly man, getting up off the grass.

'Erm, I need to phone my Dad ... to come and get me ... I ... I got a bit lost. Erm ... he'll be getting worried.'

'What's happened to you?' he asked, looking at my scratched limbs and torn shirt.

The woman walked over. 'You look like you need a drink son. Here, take this.' She held out a beaker of lemonade and, without bothering to answer the man's question, I almost snatched it off her before downing it in one go. I can still remember that taste even now; the sharp sweetness hit the roof of my mouth and the cool liquid coursed its way down my aching throat. I've never tasted anything else quite like it since. She filled the beaker up again, amid shouts of '*Oy, save some for me*' and '*Hey, don't give it all away*' and throwing me a wink, she told me to take my time with this one. Then she offered me a sandwich and self-consciously I took one, aware now that all eyes were on me waiting for an explanation. But I wasn't about to give one. It all looked so inviting; it would've been so easy and so wonderful to rest my weary body on the grass, to drink yet another beaker of cool, fresh lemonade.

'So, could you tell me where I can find a phone please? How far is Whitesands?' I asked.

'Not too far boy,' said the man. 'You on your own?'

'Erm ... yeah! Listen, I'd better be off ... thanks for the food.' I directed my reply to the woman.

'Come on, there's a phone at the farm,' she said, 'it's a lot closer than Whitesands. Come back with me. You can wait for your Dad at the house.'

She turned towards the burly man, 'I'll take the bike and bring it back out later. It'll save walking

'... and anyhow, he doesn't look like he can walk another step.' She flicked her head at me as she spoke.

The man shrugged, not entirely happy by the look on his face, while the others watched in silence. I got the impression he was the boss. I hadn't noticed a red motorbike near the gate into the field, one of those funny fat three-wheelers. I followed after her and slid onto the back seat.

We bumped our way across two more fields before I caught sight of a white farmhouse nestling in amongst the trees. I wondered how many other houses with phones I might have missed on my mad dash along the coast path. She parked the bike in a yard at the back of the house and jumped off with ease. She looked at me with warm brown eyes, wisps of hair curling round her face, and in an unwelcome rush of pain, I suddenly missed Mum. I felt my eyes well up and turned away quickly. I didn't want any more questions.

I followed the woman inside and she paused to slide a large black kettle onto the stove, before showing me into another small room. It was a sort of office. A large desk was littered with stacks of paperwork and old books, and on the wall was a large pegboard to which there were pinned dozens of cards and phone numbers scrawled on scraps of paper. On a table to the side there was a black telephone and a pile of telephone directories and other books. The woman pointed to it.

'Help yourself.' she said, 'I'll make some tea. Then you can tell me all about yourself while you wait for your Dad.'

I heaved a sigh of relief as she left the room. Then I picked up the phone, knowing this was going to be the hardest call I would ever have to make.

Chapter 16

'Dad, it's me. Listen, I haven't got much time ...'

'Joe! How's the campi ...'

'Dad, listen! Just listen! Dad, you've got to help.'

'Joe, what's going on?'

'DAD, LISTEN! Get M, and then ... listen Dad, you have to get a van, a big one ... and some blankets. Oh, and Dad, the van ... no windows, no windows in the van.'

'What? Joe, what is this ... some sort of ...'

'No, Dad ... Dad please just do it. Trust me, Dad. Listen, Dad ... find M and Jasper ... Jasper Barrow, he's the keeper at the castle ... tell them to tell you everything. Tell them I trust you ... they'll know what I mean. Then come to Whitesands Bay ... Dad, please, be as quick as you can ... today ... it's important. Dad, I can't tell you everything over the phone. Listen to M, she'll explain. It's near St. Davids ... I'll be here waiting ... Dad?'

There was a long silence in which I could hardly breathe.

'Dad ...?'

'Joe, listen, is this some sort of joke, because ...'

'No, Dad, no ... you have to help ... Dad?'

'Okay … Joe, I don't know … look, I'll try. You know I haven't …' his voice trailed off.

'Dad, I know … I know. But Dad you can do this. Dad, please try … please?' I realized I was sobbing now, 'Dad, you have to come …'

'Okay, okay. Joe … listen I'll get there somehow … Whitesands Bay, you say. I don't know it … I'll find it son, I'll find it.' Then as an afterthought, his voiced cracked, 'Joe? Joe, take care son.'

'Can you hurry … please Dad? And Dad, can you bring the kayak … we're going to need it … and water … Dad, bring some fresh water will you?'

'Joe, this is sounding more and more …'

'Dad just do as I say. Please Dad, bring the kayak.'

'Okay, okay son.'

There was a silence for a moment.

'Dad?'

'Joe?'

'Thanks … thanks Dad.'

I put the phone down quietly, hoping the woman hadn't heard my side of a very strange conversation. As an afterthought I took some change out of my pocket and placed it by the phone. Even though I would probably never see her again, it seemed important that she didn't think badly of me. Gently I tiptoed from the room and turned away from the kitchen. I slipped down a passageway and found the front door. Then like a flash, my aches and pains forgotten, I headed down a lane until I reached the farm gate with its name-plate, *Middle Hill Farm,* and then I was out on a narrow road. Without stopping I took a left for what would surely take me to Whitesands.

After the food and drink I felt loads better. I kept to a steady pace in the shade of the trees wherever I could. About twenty minutes later I saw a small sign for Whitesands, half-hidden by bushes, and taking another left turn the lane began to slope down towards the sea. I tried to stop myself from worrying; I had to believe the two dragons were okay.

It was nearing late afternoon when I saw a long sweep of sand before me. The car park was half full. There were a few families dotted along the beach and groups of surfers huddled round their camper vans waiting for the next wave. One by one they began to drift away. It was hard but all I could do was sit it out and wait. I tried not to fret about Gerald. I hoped he had as much trust in me as I had in him. I bought a bottle of pop and a Kit-Kat and another supply of biscuits from a small wooden shack on the hill just as it was closing for the day. From there I had a good view of the road and the car park and I sat in the shade, my back against the warm wood, and I rested ... I knew I was going to need all my strength and wits about me before the day was done.

I wondered where Dad was right now. This would be a huge ordeal for him; I couldn't imagine what he would be feeling like.

I don't know how many times I glanced at my watch as first six o'clock, then seven, came and went. Eventually I couldn't sit still any longer; I began to walk up and down the car park. It was almost empty now, but I was wary of drawing attention to myself, so I went back to the shack and tried to stay put. It was no good. At a quarter past seven I decided to look for a phone and was just approaching the last solitary surfer packing up his gear, when coming over the brow of the hill I saw the top of a white van. My heart leapt and I turned and ran back towards the road.

Dad threw open the van door almost before it had stopped, falling on me in a bear-like hug and almost crushing me. His face looked white and strained and his hands shook as he opened the back door. M popped her head out with a funny little smile, as if she too would like to hug me. Jasper clambered awkwardly from the passenger seat and he clasped my hands warmly and patted me on the back. I was almost overcome with relief to see them. Tears pricked my eyes and I realized how hopeless and alone I had felt all day.

We sat on the grass and Jasper poured out mugs of tea from a battered green flask while I explained exactly what had happened. I told them about Gerald swimming off, finding the other dragon, and worst of all, I described her horrible injuries. There was silence as everyone digested this information. But there was a chance we could get both of the dragons safely back and I told them how I planned to do it. Everyone looked worried, especially Dad, but after talking it over they all agreed there was no other way. It felt good to have Dad on our side; to have everything out in the open, knowing that when we got back there'd be no more secrets between us.

Chapter 17

Once we'd made up our minds we wasted no time. We unloaded the kayak from the back of the van and Dad produced two life jackets. I smiled as I put mine on, thinking he would have had forty fits if he'd seen me strapped to Gerald's back that night of the storm. M and Jasper watched as we pushed off from the sand. We were novices, it's true, but there was barely a ripple on the water that night.

We rounded the headland and headed left. I kept my eyes peeled for the narrow opening to the cave. I had no real idea how far I'd travelled along the cliff path. We approached several caves before we came to the right one; I recognized the way the rocks were formed in a tight clump, over which I'd had to scramble. We approached cautiously, my heart in my mouth and praying the two dragons would still be there. Dad pulled in the kayak as I clambered on to the little shingly beach, bigger now that the tide was further out. If they were still there Gerald would hear us. I called softly at the entrance to the cave, my voice echoing eerily and almost immediately Gerald's face appeared. I threw my arms around his neck and rubbed his face. I looked round at Dad standing behind me on the sand, his mouth open in disbelief. It had completely slipped my mind that he hadn't seen Gerald till now and I remembered how I'd felt the first time I'd seen him.

There was no sign of the other dragon. I motioned towards the sea to show what I wanted Gerald to do. He turned back towards the cave. I followed Gerald inside before Dad could stop me, and he had no choice but to follow too.

It was getting dark. There was that old familiar cave smell, salty and damp. Gradually our eyes adjusted. The dragon lay against a rock, its head resting on the gritty floor of the cave. It was panting badly and its tail looked swollen. Dad hurried back to the kayak for a bottle of water. The dragon looked at me with sad eyes and I lifted its head as Dad dribbled the water onto its parched tongue. It showed no fear; it was too weak now even for that. Patiently we trickled water down its throat and I couldn't help thinking how much better M would be at this than me.

But it was enough. Gerald licked at the dragon's face and pushed it gently with his snout and after a few more minutes it struggled to its feet. I had no idea how strong it was or even if it would be able to swim at all, but it was the only chance; if the dragon stayed here it would die for sure; we had to try. I caught Dad's eye and I smiled at him. I wanted to tell him how brilliant he'd been, but this wasn't the time or the place. It could wait.

Dad paddled out a little way first, checking there were no fishing boats nearby, but the sea and the beach were deserted now as darkness began to fall. Gerald led the way, stopping every few steps to make sure the injured dragon was following. It limped slowly across the sand and I walked alongside encouraging every step. The dragon hesitated at the water's edge and I wondered if it was remembering the helicopters, the searchlights and all the boats. We would never know what had happened, or how it came by those injuries. The dragon slipped into the sea behind Gerald and I could see how painful it was as it tried to move through the water. It couldn't use its tail as Gerald did, like a rudder to steer himself along. Instead it relied upon its wings to sweep itself through the water with feeble strokes, and I wondered if it would survive the journey home. Gerald never strayed from its side, but nudged the dragon gently along each time it faltered.

The light had almost gone now and a transparent moon drifted across a candy-striped sky. After what seemed an age we rounded the corner into the bay. The dragons kept their heads low in the water, keeping on the outside of the kayak as we approached the shore. I motioned to Gerald to stay put while Dad and I dragged the kayak on to the sand. M and Jasper hurried to help. We were all nervously double-checking that there was no one around before it felt safe enough for Dad to start up the van and move it as close to the water's edge as he dared. The last thing we needed now was to find ourselves stuck in the soft sand.

I waded out into the waves and beckoned to Gerald. The other dragon followed slowly, hauling itself out of the water with difficulty. I was afraid of hurting it but it seemed to trust me now, watching me with great sad eyes as I urged it towards the van.

M busied herself making a bed of blankets in the back of the van. Slowly and painfully we helped the injured dragon climb inside. It almost filled up the space and I knew it was going to be a squash getting Gerald in as well. He was standing out on the grass now at the side of the car park, in full view of anyone who might appear. I began to panic, remembering all those tents on the cliff top. It was only a matter of time before they would be back again.

Suddenly, before I had a chance to push Gerald into the van, there came a shout from across the car park. We all looked up in horror as a young woman came running towards us followed by a man with a camera slung over his shoulder. He began to wave it wildly in the air, while she ran ahead shouting. I think it was the noise that panicked Gerald. Before

I could stop him he made a dash for the cliff path. I shoved Dad towards the driver's door.

'Get in,' I yelled, then spinning round, 'Jasper, Jasper go!'

I pushed Jasper towards the other side of the van.

'There's a farm ... in a little valley ... *Middle Hill Farm*, it's not far, on the way to St. Justinian,' I couldn't breathe, as with one eye I watched Gerald stumbling up the cliff path, 'Just find it, I'll be there ... hurry! Hurry!' I yelled at the top of my voice. I turned towards M. 'Get in,' I yelled at her, ready to close the back doors.

'No,' she shouted, 'not this time ... I'm coming with you!' And with that she yanked the doors from my hand and slammed them closed, banging on them to let Dad know he could go. He took off at break neck speed, careering across the sand and up the slipway while we raced after Gerald.

I glanced over my shoulder. The woman was gaining on us. My aching leg muscles screamed as we clambered up onto the path. Quickly I turned back just in time to see the van shooting over the top of the hill and out of sight. And then we were running, running for our lives. Before long we caught up with Gerald. He was shivering with fear in a clump of bushes at the side of the path. We pushed him on. I could hear the sound of footsteps scraping along the path behind us and I knew they were gaining ground. Gerald was slow, he was big and cumbersome on the narrow path and he lumbered along awkwardly. And he was frightened; so frightened. I wished he would turn his fiery breath on them, but I guess no one had ever taught him to use that in anger. As far as he was concerned he was just good at lighting fires.

'They're gaining on us,' I yelled in desperation.

'I know,' said M breathlessly.

Then suddenly she came to a sharp stop in front of me and I almost knocked her flying. We were looking down over a sheer cliff face and the sea lay in a shining silver sheet below.

'Wait … stop! I've got an idea,' she cried.

M looked at Gerald, and then holding his wing she led him gently towards the edge. I held my breath and watched, as she positioned herself close beside him. He watched her in his usual intelligent way, his head on one side. Then she began to flap her arms and make diving motions. I stood back, watching. I didn't much like what I saw. Gerald seemed bewildered and shuffled back onto the path, though I think he understood what she meant him to do. M prodded him back towards the edge again. She wasn't taking no for an answer.

'You can do it Gerald. I know you can … you were meant to fly. It's not far, just a little way, and then you can dive down into the water … just like a bird.'

Gerald looked back at her, his eyes deep and troubled. M stroked his face gently.

'Go on Gerald … fly. Fly home. We'll be there waiting for you,' her voice was soft, her eyes begging him. 'Go Gerald,' she whispered.

And I found myself muttering, 'Fly Gerald … fly!'

Suddenly there was a shout from behind. The photographer and the woman were standing just yards away. He had the camera poised while she stood with her mouth wide open.

'Go Gerald, go. NOW,' M screamed and with that she pushed him clean off the cliff top. I closed my eyes in horror. I couldn't look. I couldn't bear to watch as Gerald crashed onto the rocks below.

'Joe, JOE … look! He's flying, Gerald's flying,' her voice was somewhere half way between tears and laughter. She grabbed my arm and I looked down and there he was, like a beautiful gleaming bird, his scales shining in the silvery light of the moon, he sped across the water, his wings flapping silently, as straight as an arrow he flew before diving deep below the surface and out of sight.

'Oh Gerald,' I whispered, 'get home safely.'

Chapter 18

I felt something grab my arm and I turned. The woman reporter held on to me while her friend tried to take a picture. I squirmed round and wrenched my arm away. She swore as I twisted away from her and taking a swipe I managed to knock the camera clean off balance. They both stared in disbelief as it flew into the air and clattered down over the rocks and into the sea below.

'Run!' I yelled.

We shot along the path, paying little attention to the spiky bushes and dangerous drop below. There was no time for that; nothing could stop us now. I thanked God when at last I recognized the hedge I had climbed over earlier that day. We pounded up the field then blundered our way through the bushes and clambered over the wooden fence. The big field was clear of bales now, but I knew it was the right one. We rushed across it and by the time we reached the gate our pursuers were just clambering over the fence. They were shouting at each other by now, an argument in full swing, and that made us laugh.

M had a pain in her side from running so we slowed down a bit, following the ruts along the side of the fields where I had ridden on the red bike. We had no breath left to talk. As we neared the farmhouse I could see lights on inside and I thought of the kind farmer's wife.

It was as we were crossing the farmyard on tiptoe that a dog ran out of the yard growling and barking like mad. We stopped dead. M quickly tried to pacify the dog in that way she has, but it wasn't working this time. Suddenly the yard was flooded in light from a rusty lamp hanging on the wall above our heads.

'You again!' said the farmer's wife; her husband glowered behind her.

'What's going on?' he growled.

I was lost for words; my newfound talent for lying had deserted me.

'I'm going to call the police,' the woman continued, an eyebrow raised at us, 'perhaps you could explain it to them?'

'Listen,' I began, 'about earlier. I mean … thanks for helping me today … it's just … I can't tell you what I'm doing here, or what this is all about. Honest, I can't. But we're not up to anything. Really, we're not.'

She didn't say anything, just stood looking at us, waiting for an explanation.

'We have to go,' I said, 'we're in a hurry. Someone's after us, we have to get away. Please …'

'After you?' Then, thoughtfully, 'Is this something to do with that dragon creature, or whatever it is?'

'Course not,' I replied as calmly as I could, 'but they're bad people ... they're after us. We can't let them ... erm ...' I shifted a few paces towards the gate, grabbing M's arm and moving her with me.

Suddenly there was the sound of footsteps and shouting as the photographer and the woman came stumbling into the yard. The farmer and his wife looked up in astonishment, while the dog went berserk, barking and yapping at their feet.

We took our chance. We ran. Out through the gate and onto the lane leaving chaos behind us. The photographer tried to follow, but the dog leapt at him fiercely. I was so tired I didn't know how much longer I could keep this up. M struggled along beside me as we fell into potholes and stumbled over stones in the darkness. But then we heard it, the unmistakable sound of an engine and moments later Dad screeched to a halt when he caught us in the glare of the headlights. As he turned the van round in a narrow gateway we tumbled into the back.

*

'You were brilliant,' I said quietly.

M turned an enquiring look my way. She was sitting with the dragon's head cradled on her lap, stroking one of its ears.

'Back there,' I flicked my head back as I said this, 'you saved him ... Gerald. If it hadn't been for you ...'

'What about you,' she replied, 'you *found* her. *That* was brilliant. And your Dad ... he was amazing.'

'Yeah ... it must've been ... really tough for him today.'

And that was when I told her. About Mum I mean. Everything.

It had been their wedding anniversary. Mum had a rare night off duty. They'd been to a film and then gone to a small Italian place she liked. I was staying at a friend's house. Dad had sat down with me the next day and explained exactly how it happened. And that was just about the last time he'd really talked about her.

They'd left the restaurant and were walking back to their car hand in hand. The streets were busy; people were on their way home. Then just as they turned the corner, two youths in a battered car pulled to a stop a few yards in front of them. They piled out and, grabbing a well-dressed man in a suit, started punching him until he fell to the ground. Then they snatched his briefcase and wallet and jumped back in the car and sped off. Mum was a sergeant in the Metropolitan Police. She couldn't just stand there and let them get away with it. She simply went into police mode, making sure that someone had telephoned for an ambulance and ordering Dad to chase after the car. He wanted to wait for the police, but she could still see the car tail-lights ahead. Mum had taken every special driving course going, but Dad was no racing driver. He tried to keep up, swerving in and out of the traffic to keep them in sight, with Mum urging him on all the way.

It happened at a set of traffic lights. They were on amber. They changed to red just as Dad sped towards the line. Mum screamed at him to keep going, but he slammed on the brakes … and the car skidded across the road, and spun round right into the path of a big red London bus. Dad escaped somehow – but she didn't stand a chance. They took her to Charing Cross Hospital. I remembered the phone ringing in my friend's house late that night. Then quiet mutterings from downstairs, then the gentle shaking on my arm. But I was already awake.

I stood at her bedside and held her hand. I like to think she knew I was there. Once I saw her eyes lightly flutter and imagined a slight pressure from her fingers. She never made it through the night though.

I didn't blame Dad, how could I? But the trouble was he blamed himself. Maybe if Mum had driven that night, things might have turned out different, but that was something we would never know. Since then Dad hadn't sat behind a steering wheel – until now, that was. Suddenly I realized that M's hand had crept inside my own. I was glad it was dark inside the van. It meant she couldn't see my face and the tears slipping silently down my cheeks. We travelled in silence for a while, each lost in our own thoughts. Then M broke the silence, and for a moment I wondered what she meant.

'Let's call her Marigold,' she whispered, looking down at the dragon.

'*Marigold*? Erm ... so it's a girl dragon?'

''Course. Don't you like it?'

'Uh ...'

M smiled sheepishly and it suddenly dawned on me where she had found a name like that.

'Well ... oh, yeah! Marigold ... yeah, why not? I guess it suits her,' I grinned. 'Nice name.'

But deep in our hearts we were both wondering if Marigold would even survive.

Once we hit the open road Dad slowed down; we needed to get home safely without any more mishaps. M told me about how her side of the plan had gone, about the decoy she and Jasper had made. Jasper had remembered seeing a small wooden boat lost amongst an overgrown patch of weeds at the bottom of his garden. They'd hacked away the undergrowth and pulled it out. Jasper had mended it with some thin pieces of wood and a sticky black substance, which he heated in an old saucepan on the stove and painted over the patch he'd made. He'd taken two old car tyres and cut them in half. They positioned three of the half-tyres upright in the bottom of the boat so that they stuck up like humps, holding them fast with wire. The last piece of tyre was screwed to the front of the boat. I was beginning to picture nothing less than the Loch Ness Monster. Then M had used an old green bedspread from her house, which she draped over the whole thing. She'd bought some thick, shiny metallic sheets from a craft shop and hoped they'd hold up in the water. She cut round scale shapes and stapled them to the blanket, so that they flapped about a little bit in the breeze.

Late one evening they'd brought the boat down to the little bay, carrying it along the passageway between them. It was hard work she said, it took all their strength. They waited until after midnight then launched it in a mad dash to the sea, hoping the tide would take it in the right direction. M smiled, remembering how real it had looked bobbing about in the moonlight. It didn't need to last long, just long enough to draw the crowds away from St. Justinian. And it had worked. I rested my head against the side of the van and thought how brilliant everyone had been.

But those thoughts were soon pushed to one side because it was hard to think of anything but Gerald. Where was he? Alone in the sea somewhere, lost? I remembered how cats and dogs have a built in instinct for getting back home and wondered if dragons had one too. Could he ever find his way back? I looked at M. She was deep in thought as she stroked Marigold's ear, and I guessed she was thinking pretty much along the same lines as me.

Chapter 19

It had been touch and go since that night. Dad drove the van through the castle gates, right up to the entrance to the dungeons. Marigold limped awkwardly to the cave and slumped down in a corner. She seemed weaker than ever.

But we used whatever means we had to save her. Dad had some tablets to help restful sleep. We gave them with some milk and M was brilliant again, coaxing Marigold to drink. And while she slept M and Jasper cleaned the blood and dirt from her wound. Jasper disappeared into the woods and came back with several mysterious plants, which he made into a sort of broth and trickled down her throat from a spoon. Then he mixed some of them into a paste and bound them around her tail. M had some antibiotics left over from treating her animals. We tripled the dose for Marigold. And slowly, miraculously, she began to recover.

A week later and we could see a change in her as she began to drink all the milk we could give her. M tempted her with baby rusks and toast. I watched with a mixture of envy and admiration as the bond between them grew. Not long after, the end of her tail fell clean off and it healed into a stubby, misshapen stump. But she was alive and getting stronger every day, and that was all that mattered.

Yet my thoughts were always with Gerald. Day after day, night after night we waited and watched, all of us, taking turns to stay with Marigold. We'd sit in the little cove, or scan the water with Dad's binoculars from the rocks above. The weather turned cold and windy and the sea was often so black and choppy we couldn't see anything. We called and called, our hands cupped round our mouths. Dad took to walking along the cliff paths. We hired a car and drove along the coast road all the way to St. Justinian, stopping dozens of times along the way. But there was no sign of Gerald.

After our escape from the reporters there'd been a big fuss in the papers again, but the whole thing soon died down. Everyone thought it was just a great big hoax. Even so, we kept an ear out for the news, just in case. I didn't think I would be able to bear it if Gerald was hunted like Marigold had been.

One good thing to come out of it all, however, was Dad. I marvelled at the change in him, at the tender way in which he helped with Marigold and at his determination in looking for Gerald. And I knew he was doing it for me. He wasn't just his old self; it was more than that. We were closer than we'd ever been and he knew how scared I was for Gerald; he wanted him back too.

Then one day Jasper and I were sitting on the cliff top above the little bay. It was early evening and the sun was ablaze on the horizon. The nights were drawing in; summer was finally coming to an end Jasper was quiet, deep in thought, having little to say. He put his hand on my arm.

'You know Joe ... it's been a long time now ...'

'Don't say that!' I whispered.

'It's over a month ... I don't know ...' his voice was so low I could hardly hear him.

'He's strong,' I cried, 'you didn't see how he swam that night, in the storm. He was so ... so ...' my voice faltered.

'I hope you're right Joe,' and he patted my hand and shook his head sadly even as the words left his mouth.

I lifted my arm against the glare of the sinking sun. My heart was sinking too with every day that passed.

Suddenly I jumped to my feet. It had been just a fleeting shape, a tail sliding through the water. I ran towards the cliff edge.

'What?' Jasper was beside me, 'Joe, did you see something?'

'I dunno ... a shape ... something ... there was something there.'

'Where? I can't see anything.'

'There! Look! It's Gerald! Jasper, he's back.'

I scrambled recklessly down onto the rocks throwing off my shirt and my shoes on the way.

'Joe ... wait! Come back!' shouted Jasper from behind. 'It might be nothing!'

But I couldn't stop. I dived into the water and swam straight in the direction I'd seen him.

'Gerald,' I whispered, breathing his name with every stroke.

I hadn't imagined it. I knew I hadn't. Back and forth I swam, barely noticing as the cold water seeped through my bones. I could see Jasper waving his arms at me from the shore, but I took no notice. I couldn't give up now. I craned my neck, searching above the swell of the waves as they sloshed and slapped their way to shore. The breeze came up and turned the sea into a frothing mass of heaving water. And I began to get tired, very tired, very quickly.

Suddenly my legs were lifeless and it felt as if I had no strength left in my arms. I trod water for a few minutes and tried to get my strength back. Gerald wasn't there. I sobbed and turned for the shore, but no matter how hard I tried I was making no headway. I was in trouble, big trouble. The water pounded against my face and little lights flickered before my eyes.

I remember going under and fighting my way back to the top, my mouth filled with the thick salty water, before I went down, down for the last time.

Chapter 20

15 years later

So, here I am, at the church gate. We are early, Dad and I. He sits on a seat across the grass from me, his thick mop of grey hair ruffling in a light summer breeze which warms my face and brings with it the smell of honeysuckle and a faint waft of the sea. From up here the village looks as if it is made up of dolls' houses, and I can't help but think back to the day we arrived here, at the tiny village of Manorbier in a far flung corner of south west Wales. That was fifteen years ago now, and I was just a boy then.

I watch as the pony and trap turns up the hill towards the church, its delicate ribbons fluttering in the air. I take her hand and she steps down from it in a froth of white lace. I see that she has plaited her hair still, but now it is wound in a knot at the nape of her neck and threaded with pearls.

It will be a small wedding. We're breaking with tradition; we'll walk down the aisle hand in hand, to our new life together. But first there's something we must do. We walk down the path and cross the grass to the little graveyard. The grave hasn't been there long, just a couple of years.

OUR DEAREST FRIEND
JASPER BARROW
DIED – 10th October 1991

I will always wonder how old he really was. We'd searched amongst the many books and documents in his cottage and in the cave. But there was nothing, no clue as to when he was born or where he came from.

I thought of the family tree Dad had done for us. He'd traced his Welsh roots way back to the 1700s, and there she was, Emily Barrow, born 1752. We couldn't find a direct connection to Jasper but I knew, had always known I think, since that first time I saw him, that we shared a tiny drop of the same blood running through our veins. I miss him badly. M takes a single white rose from her bouquet and places it on the grave.

From where we stand we can look across the valley to the castle and I catch her smile. We never tire of looking after our two friends there, and if it hadn't been for Gerald I wouldn't be here now. It was he who scooped me from the water with his tail that day and brought me safely ashore. I don't remember anything. When I came round I was lying in the mouth of the cave, coughing up water, Gerald watching over me.

I imagine the two of them, sitting there now

in their cave like a funny old couple and I wonder what the future holds for them – and for us all. Dad has taken over the post of caretaker and he moved into Jasper's cottage a few months ago. I feel so proud of him, and he of me too I think. Sometimes I wonder if he's lonely, but he has a new purpose in life now and he seems contented. We still miss Mum of course, but it's different, because now we talk about her and remember the things she used to say and do.

M starts her job at the local vets next week. What else would she do? And me? Well, I took a degree in History and Environmental Science. I'm training to be a National Park Warden. I've grown to love these coastal waters and I want to protect the wildlife around them.

And while I'm out there I'll keep an eye out for a flash of gleaming tail … just in case.

About Diane...

I was born and brought
up in Manorbier,
Pembrokeshire, where this
book is set. I still live in
the area, just a few miles
away, and I love walking
along the spectacular
Pembrokeshire beaches and
clifftops with my dog, Tess.

I've always enjoyed writing. Even as a child, I was
scribbling stories in my spare time – probably the
only thing I was really good at through school! But I
went on to work as a finance manager though – and
writing became my spare time passion.

I wrote this novel originally for my two daughters
as a good bedtime read, and it was inspired by the
places I explored as a child – seashores, caves, cliffs
and castles. I love this area – it's full of beauty and
a sense of mystery and discovery. I hope that comes
through in my book.

I have seven grandchildren to keep me busy, but
I enjoy cooking and walking – and reading too, of
course! I hope this book inspires you to visit the
places which were a part of Joe and M's story.